AVENGER IN TRAINING

"The real wild card in this deck is Justis McFain," Longarm said.

"He's paralyzed. Probably in a wheelchair."

"I know, Luke, but don't be fooled into thinking he can't shoot and kill us."

"Anything else I should know?"

"Only that you're forcing me to take you into a situation where you do not belong," Longarm said flatly. "It's one that could get you killed."

Luke's cheeks reddened, and he said hotly, "I'm telling you that I've decided to be a lawman!"

"More stubborn than a damned Missouri mule," Longarm muttered. He'd have to watch the cowboy real close, or the fool kid was going to get them into one helluva gun battle.

TABOR EVANS

LONGARM

ON A BLOODY VENDETTA

JOVE BOOKS, NEW YORK

LONGARM ON A BLOODY VENDETTA

A Jove Book / published by arrangement with
the author

PRINTING HISTORY
Jove edition / October 2000

All rights reserved.
Copyright © 2000 by Penguin Putnam Inc.
This book may not be reproduced in whole or in part,
by mimeograph or any other means, without permission.
For information address: The Berkley Publishing Group,
a division of Penguin Putnam Inc.,
375 Hudson Street, New York, New York 10014.

The Penguin Putnam Inc. World Wide Web site address is
http://www.penguinputnam.com

ISBN: 0-515-12932-1

A JOVE BOOK®
Jove Books are published by The Berkley Publishing Group,
a division of Penguin Putnam Inc.,
375 Hudson Street, New York, New York 10014.
JOVE and the "J" design
are trademarks belonging to Penguin Putnam Inc.

PRINTED IN THE UNITED STATES OF AMERICA

10 9 8 7 6 5 4 3 2 1

Chapter 1

Deputy Marshal Custis Long and the tall, strikingly beautiful brunette on his arm crossed Denver's busy Colfax Avenue, passed the U.S. Mint, and finally came to a halt before the huge sandstone Federal Building.

"Are you sure you can do this?" Elizabeth Bonner asked, her brow furrowing with concern as she gazed up at the man she loved. "You don't have to hand over your badge, Custis. Not unless you really want to."

"I've agonized over this decision for months," Longarm finally replied. "And while I'm going to miss the excitement of being a federal marshal, it's not any kind of life for a married man. You know how much I travel and the dangerous men I have hunted and sometimes had to kill."

"Yes, but . . ."

"Elizabeth," he said, gently placing a forefinger over her protesting lips. "We're going to be married. It's not something I planned or really ever expected, but now that it is about to happen, I couldn't be happier."

"Me neither." The woman sighed. "This is amazing, considering how after my horrible first marriage, I swore never to fall in love again. And I was content with loving only my son and enjoying our life out on Father's ranch.

Then . . . then you came along, and suddenly everything changed."

Longarm looked deep into her lovely green eyes and boldly drew her into his arms, unaware of the envious attention they were getting from passersby. "Changed for the better, I hope."

"You know it has." Elizabeth kissed his lips, then smiled. "My life has suddenly taken on new meaning. I have never been so much in love."

"Me neither," he told her. "And the idea of being away from you for months at a time just isn't to my liking. Besides, you'd be worrying all the time about my health and safety."

"Yes," she admitted, "I would. But, if you really must be a lawman, then I'd never want to take that away from you."

"I'll have a big challenge learning the cattle business from scratch," he said. "It might not be quite as exciting as hunting down fugitives of the law, but there will be other rewards . . . like being home every night, sleeping under a roof with you in my arms, and watching your son grow to be a man."

"And maybe having sons and daughters of *our* making too," she whispered, cheeks coloring slightly. "That is, if God is willing."

"I can't answer for God, but *I* sure am willing."

Elizabeth's cheeks colored even more deeply. "You are quite a catch. I imagine that dozens of pretty young women all over the West are going to be crying their eyes out when they discover that we've become man and wife."

"As will a lot of successful young bachelors in this town," he told her. "Why, you should hear the gossip that is going on up in the office."

"Really?"

Custis nodded. "Ever since the day that I brought you up to meet my boss, the tongues have been endlessly wagging. I'd never brought a woman up to meet Billy Vail

2

before, so everyone knew you were pretty special."

"And now I'm going to take you away from them. They're not going to be very happy about losing a man of your caliber."

"They'll survive," Longarm told her. "Every year they recruit new federal law officers, and they seem to find enough to meet their quotas."

"Perhaps," Elizabeth said, "but a special man like yourself doesn't come along very often. That's why I'm putting a ring on your finger and taking your name."

Longarm grinned broadly. How had he ever gotten so lucky? Not only was he getting a beautiful bride, but a fine eleven-year-old son and a new life learning to become a successful cattle rancher on one of the finest operations in Colorado.

The Bonner Ranch owned more than sixty thousand acres of prime grazing land and nearly ten thousand head of cattle. Clyde Bonner and Elizabeth's mother had homesteaded the land and built it up until their ranch was second to none in the territory. They'd survived eight winters in a sod dugout before there'd been enough money to build an impressive two-story house and begin a family. But even then life had been hard, and they'd lost an earlier daughter and a son before Elizabeth had come along. Now, Clyde's health was failing and Elizabeth, being the only heir, would soon inherit the Bonner Ranch. And Custis Longarm, a man who had never accumulated any kind of wealth and who had never settled down, was about to assume the job of ranch manager over a bunch of cowboys who probably knew more than he'd ever know about raising cattle.

Sure, I'm getting a late start, but dammit, Longarm thought, I can learn as well as any man.

"Just think," Elizabeth said, fairly bouncing with joy, "we are going to be wed in only two weeks!"

"I can't wait," he replied. "It's time for me to settle down and start building something for the future."

Longarm removed his badge and cradled it in his big hand. "But I have to say that I have enjoyed being a federal lawman. I've been so many places and met all kinds of people . . . most of them good, but a few real bad. The memories of being a marshal will stick with me a long, long time."

"Just as long as they don't include all the women you've met and made love to," Elizabeth said with mock seriousness. "The past is the past. Now, we just need to concentrate on the future and keep building what Father and Mother started."

"I'll do my level best," he promised.

She squeezed his hand. "That's all I'll ever ask or expect, Custis. I know that this isn't an easy transition for you and that it will be terribly hard to go up there now and hand in your resignation. But I'll do everything I can to make sure that it's a decision that you never regret."

Longarm knew that Elizabeth wasn't exaggerating. He'd met and dallied with a hell of a lot of beautiful women in his time and travels, but this one was the most sincere and loving and wonderful of them all. Miss Elizabeth Grayson Bonner could have chosen far more successful men, but she'd picked him . . . a fella who didn't have more than a couple of dollars squirreled away in the bank for a rainy day. Longarm owned no house, no horse, no saddle, and sometimes he didn't even seem to have much good sense . . . but Elizabeth loved him just the same.

Just how lucky can a man get? he asked himself one more time.

"Go on," Elizabeth said. "I'll be up the street shopping and I'll meet you back here in . . . what?"

"Ten minutes will do."

"Nonsense! Now, you just break the news to Mr. Vail as gently as you can."

"He won't be happy."

"But I will be."

"Yeah. I expect he might even offer me a desk job."

4

"You'd hate that!" Elizabeth exclaimed.

"True."

"Just tell Mr. Vail that you are leaving but that you'd be honored if he would stand in as your best man. That will make him feel pretty proud."

"It will," Longarm agreed. "But he'll still be upset. You see, they're real shorthanded now and . . ."

"Custis, are you changing your mind?" Elizabeth asked. "Because, if you are . . . well, it's all right."

"No," he said with finality. "I'm resigning today. Billy will just have to take it like a man and the agency will need to get off its duff and hire my replacement."

"Good! That's the stuff. You just tell him and then ask him to be your best man, and then hand over your badge. It won't be all that hard."

Longarm wasn't so sure, but he nodded. "Okay. I'll meet you here in an hour?"

"How about two hours? I can't do much shopping in less time. And you know, I don't get this opportunity very often. Why, I'm here to pick my wedding dress, among other things, and I sure don't want to be hurried."

"Okay, two hours," he agreed. "There's always some paperwork to be done. I hate it, but don't want to leave a stack of reports to my replacement."

Elizabeth kissed him one more time, and then hurried off with a wave of her hand. Longarm watched her proceed up Colfax, and he couldn't help but admire the view. There were several other men admiring Elizabeth's backside as well, and that caused Longarm's hands to momentarily knot into fists, but then he realized he couldn't blame other men for enjoying such a fine sight.

Just as long as they look but don't touch, he thought as he turned and headed up the stairs into the Federal Building with a mounting sense of dread. Dread because he and Billy Vail went back a long ways together and breaking this news to his old friend, mentor, and boss was going to be worse than pulling teeth.

● ● ●

"Come on in!" Billy shouted.

Longarm opened the door, and his boss smiled a greeting. Billy didn't stand up or extend his hand. They were too close and familiar with each other to go through any such foolish formalities.

"You got a minute, Billy?"

"For you? Of course! Come on in and have a seat. I was just about to hunt you down anyway."

"You were?"

"That's right. You ever heard of Copper Creek?"

"Sure, it's a small mining and ranching town about twenty miles west of Pueblo. Nice country."

"That's right. Well, the marshal down there has a couple of murderers cooling their heels in his jail. He sent a telegram asking for us to come down and pick them up. They're wanted for gunning down two federal mail employees on the northbound train. You remember what a gruesome scene that was last year."

"Yeah," Longarm said bitterly. "They tortured those fellas for hours trying to get them to open the safe. They'd learned that it contained a rare shipment of gold and jewelry, as I remember."

"That's right." Billy's smile died. "They really worked those two men over before they finally gave up the safe's combination. Then, they shot both men between the eyes! The bloody bastards sure as hell didn't need to do that."

"They thought the postal workers were the only witnesses," Longarm said. "But it turned out there were several others that had seen them leave the mail car when it arrived here in Denver. I hope they swing."

"Oh," Billy said, "they will."

"How'd the marshal in a little place like Copper Creek manage to capture and jail such a dangerous pair?"

Marshal Billy Vail was a short, stocky man in contrast to Longarm, who stood six feet four in his stocking feet. Vail had a receding hairline and a bulging waistline, but

6

he was a bulldog when it came to seeking justice and retribution. Now, he picked up a telegram from his desk and read it again.

"The marshal's name is Potter. Amos T. Potter. All he says in this telegram is that he caught them naked and blind drunk while they were enjoying themselves in one of the local whorehouses." Billy shrugged. "I guess he got real lucky."

"Are they wanted for anything else?"

"Potter doesn't say if they are or not. I guess he just wants them out of his jail and brought before a judge up here in Denver. But I get the feeling they are really a handful. That's why I want you to take the Denver and Rio Grande down there first thing tomorrow morning and bring them back in manacles. Don't take any chances, just—"

"Wait a minute." Longarm put up a hand.

"What's wrong?"

"I can't accept this assignment."

Billy's jaw dropped. "Why the hell not?"

"I . . . I'm getting married."

"Well, I'll be a ringtailed polecat! Congratulations!" Billy's round face was all smiles again. "You and Miss Bonner are a perfect match. I was telling my wife just the other day that I've never seen you happier than you've been since you met that lovely lady. Custis, this is great news!"

"Well," Longarm hedged, "you haven't heard all of it, I'm afraid."

Billy's grin faded. "You're not thinking of quitting the agency . . . are you?"

"I've been thinking of it for weeks and that's exactly what I have in mind."

"But—"

"Listen," Longarm said, cutting him off. "You know how hard it is for a couple to be married while the husband is off all the time chasing outlaws. Why, you told me your-

7

self that having a family was the most important thing in the world and that it just didn't mix with being a federal manhunter."

"Yeah, I said that, but . . ."

"It wouldn't be fair to Elizabeth or to her son, Josh. The kid needs a real father. He's never had the pleasure of being taught anything but how to cowboy. Old Clyde Bonner adores the kid, but being a grandfather isn't the same as being a father. Josh is long overdue for a father."

"But you *aren't* his father and you never will be."

Longarm frowned and chose his words with care. "I know that, but I'll be the best he never had, if that makes any sense. His real father never gave him a minute. Josh needs me at the ranch. You should hear him talk about all the things we could do together, starting with fishing and hunting."

Billy leaned back in his chair and sighed. "So you've come to hand over your badge, huh?"

"I'm afraid so."

"Damn! There is no way that I can replace you. It takes years for a man to learn what you know . . . if he lives that long. Custis, I really am sorry about this decision."

"Well, at least you know how much I enjoyed working for you and being a deputy marshal."

"What if I were to tell you," Billy asked, eyes narrowing, "that I have asked for you to be promoted?"

"You have?"

"That's right. I should have done it a long, long time ago. But the paperwork has been submitted and I think your promotion is as good as done."

"Thanks," Longarm said, "but it's too little too late and doesn't change anything."

"You'd get more money, and most likely you'd work here in the Federal Building. Elizabeth would like that. So how does it sound?"

"Awful. I couldn't handle the politics or sitting behind

a desk. I appreciate your trying to get me a promotion, but I'm finished here."

"When is the wedding?" Billy asked with a sigh of futility.

"Two weeks. And I'd like you to be my best man."

"I'd be honored. And I really am happy for you and Miss Bonner . . . the kid too. But I have a favor to ask. Just a small one."

"Anything."

Billy stood up. "I need you to go down there and bring those two murderers back for trial. It won't take but three days . . . four at the most. Will you do that for me, Custis? I don't have anyone else in the office that I'd trust to return a pair as bad as these two. I'd go myself but I've got bureaucrats pouring in from Washington, and I'm expected to be here when they arrive. So can I count on you for this one small and final favor?"

"Sure," Longarm said, knowing it would make things more difficult both for Elizabeth and himself, but that it was the least he could do for this good friend.

"Thanks," Billy said with obvious relief.

"I'll leave for Copper Creek on the train tomorrow morning."

"Marshal Potter will be happy to hear that, and I'll send him off a telegram with the good news this afternoon."

Billy sat down and stared at the stack of papers on his desk. "I really envy you," he said without looking up at his best deputy marshal. "Overnight, you go from a low-paid man-hunter to a cattle rancher. And not just any cattle rancher, but one of the most prosperous in Colorado."

"Our marriage changes nothing in regard to my lack of wealth. The title to the ranch will remain the same," Longarm explained. "It will still belong to Mr. Bonner, who will pass it down to Elizabeth . . . not me."

"Sure," Billy said, making it clear he didn't believe that to be the case. "How are you going to learn to punch cattle instead of outlaw faces?"

"I know a thing or two about horses and cattle."

Billy scoffed. "You know how to ride a horse. I'll grant you that. But cattle? Hell, Custis, you don't know a thing about the beasts except that you like them cooked medium-rare!"

Longarm had to laugh. Then he asked, "How tough can handling a cow be after handling all the cutthroats and killers I've had to deal with all these past years?"

"Good point." Billy picked up a pencil and began to fidget. "Listen, Custis, I've got a couple of reports due. I'd better get back to work."

"Then I'll see you in a few days," Longarm said, backing toward the office door. "And thanks for agreeing to be my best man."

"My pleasure. And Custis?"

"Yeah?"

"Be very careful."

"Don't worry. I'm always careful."

"Yeah, but this time, be extra careful. I'm worried that you might have your mind on more . . . more pleasant things than your prisoners. Because, if your mind wanders for even a second, these outlaws will somehow find a way to kill you."

"I've had tougher assignments."

"I know, but you've never had so much to lose."

"Meaning?"

"It might change you."

"How?"

Billy shrugged. "You could let your mind wander and get careless. These outlaws have nothing to lose, and they know they'll swing when they get back here. They'll be desperate, and if you get careless for even—"

"My mind won't wander," Longarm vowed. "And I never get careless."

"I'm glad to hear that. Say hello to Miss Bonner and offer her my most heartfelt congratulations."

"I'll do it," Longarm promised as he was leaving.

10

Chapter 2

"Oh, Custis!" Elizabeth cried, rushing toward him and nearly knocking over an old street peddler in the process. "I can't wait to show you my wedding dress! I like it so much."

"Then why didn't you buy it?" he asked, pulling her close.

"I needed to make sure that you approved. You might not like it."

"I'm sure that I will. Honey," he said, "you could wear a serape to our wedding and I'd still think you the most beautiful bride ever."

"You're sweet. But I really want you to see it on me first."

When she started to drag him down the street toward a dress shop, Longarm stood his ground, saying, "Elizabeth, I've got something to tell you."

Her brown eyes widened with shock and alarm. "Did you change your mind about resigning?"

"No."

"Then what . . ."

"Billy begged me to accept one more small assignment."

"How small?"

"Very. I just have to take the train down to Pueblo tomorrow, then ride over to Copper Creek and collect a couple of fugitives."

"That's it?"

"That's it," he told her. "No big deal."

"Custis, if it's no 'big deal,' then why couldn't Mr. Vail find someone else to do the job? Or even do it himself? He is qualified to do that sort of thing, isn't he?"

"Of course. But he has meetings with some Washington officials, and I think he's probably gone a little soft."

"What are you talking about?"

"Nothing." Longarm felt a small trickle of sweat working its way down his backbone. "It's just that these two prisoners are kind of rough."

"You mean dangerous."

"That's right."

Elizabeth took a deep breath. "What are they accused of?"

"Murder. They're probably the robbers that killed those two mail clerks on the train last year."

"And *tortured* them!" Elizabeth was upset. "Custis, I read all about those gruesome killings. The perpetrators must be men without souls."

"They're in jail under heavy guard. I'll handcuff them and put ankle chains on both. It's an easy assignment, and I'll be back here in just a couple of days."

"Can you promise me this will be the very last assignment you get talked into accepting?"

"You have my promise."

"And that you will be *very* careful?"

"Yes, very careful."

"And come back to marry me?"

"Of course."

He felt her shudder. Then Elizabeth raised her head and managed to smile. "Forgive me for being so nervous. It's just that now, after finally finding you, I couldn't bear to lose you. Not ever."

Longarm held her close. "I feel exactly the same way. Now, shall we go take a look at that wedding dress?"

She surprised him when she shook her head. "I'd rather wait until you return."

"I understand. Are you hungry?"

"For you," she said brazenly. "Instead of heading back to the ranch this afternoon, let's find a hotel room."

Longarm was shocked because they hadn't yet made love. Elizabeth was a bit old-fashioned and . . . well, they'd agreed to wait until their wedding night. Actually, Longarm had found the anticipation to be deep and satisfying. But now . . . now she was changing her mind.

"Are you sure?"

"Very."

"But why?"

"I don't know," she said, looking right into his eyes. "I just have a feeling that we shouldn't put off anything else."

A slow smile formed on Longarm's lips. "That's fine with me. I know a hotel where they are very discreet."

"I thought you might."

Longarm was at a loss for the words needed to undo his mistake, so he stammered, "Oh, hell, let's find someplace that I've never been before."

"I'd like that," she told him. "And I know such a hotel."

"You do?"

"Yes. It's the one that my father and I stay at when we come to town."

"But they'll all *know* you."

"Of course. But I'll register in my name. You can sneak around to the alley and take the stairs up to the second landing, where I'll unlock the door and be waiting."

"Sneaky."

"And exciting," she told him as they hurried away.

The Rutherford Hotel was one of the most elegant in Denver, and the staff practically fell over themselves trying to be helpful the moment that they recognized Clyde Bonner's daughter. Longarm struggled to suppress a grin as he waved to Elizabeth and headed around the building, then to the alley. It was empty, and he wasted no time in scrambling up the stairs, where Elizabeth awaited with open arms.

"This is so deceitful and so delicious," she breathed, leading him down the richly carpeted hallway and into a suite that was fit for royalty with its own chandelier and beautiful four-poster bed carved in Spain.

"My God," he said, "when you and your father come to town, you really live it up!"

"We supply this hotel with its beef, and in return, they treat us rather special. This room, for example, costs us very little. And," she added, "it even comes with a fully stocked bar."

"Is this the room you stay in?"

"Oh, no," she said with a giggle, "mine is much smaller. This is Father's room, but I slipped Andre, the man in charge downstairs, a little extra cash and discreetly informed him I wanted it for myself."

"And he didn't suspect the reason?"

"Andre might suspect . . . but he'd never tell . . . even if he was sure we were having a lovers' tryst." Elizabeth pirouetted and then began to unbutton her dress. "Well, what do you think?"

"I think that our real wedding night is going to have to go a long way to beat what we are about to enjoy."

"Then hold back just a little," she teased. "And I'll try to do the same."

"Not a chance!"

Then they were tearing off their clothes and jumping into bed. Longarm had thought he could take his future wife slowly, but they were both so filled with excitement that they could not wait to share a little foreplay. And besides, they'd already been doing that for several weeks, and so when Elizabeth whispered, "Please, just get inside

14

of me now and make me feel like your woman!" Longarm was all too ready to oblige.

He mounted her swiftly, and soon they were both lunging and gasping, straining and pulling each other closer as their passion rose to a feverish level.

"Oh, Liz," he groaned, feeling the fire in his belly start to burn its way down into his testicles. "I'm afraid I can't hold back with you very long this time."

"Then don't," she cried, legs wrapping around the small of his back as she pumped joyously and raked his back with her fingernails. "Come on! Give it all to me now!"

Longarm lost himself in his bride-to-be. He went crazy with lust and love, and soon they were both screaming with ecstasy as their bodies surrendered the last semblance of conscious control. Longarm felt his seed exploding into Elizabeth's body, and he felt her stiffen and convulse in a series of powerful jerks. When it was over, they collapsed and lay locked in each other's arms.

"My heavens," she panted, "when we do this thing really right we're probably going to kill each other."

"I know," he replied. "I've never had one so strong."

"I never had one at all," she confessed, hugging his neck and wiping her tears on his shoulder. "Oh, Custis, you are everything I ever dreamed that a man should be."

"I'll try to stay that way," he said, his voice thick with emotion. "I really will."

"And you'll always love me?"

"Always."

"That's all I need to hear. That, and how you'll soon be coming back to me."

"Nothing can stop that," he promised.

Elizabeth sighed and closed her eyes. She fell asleep, and Longarm watched her for a long, long time before he fell asleep as well. Sometime after midnight, they roused into wakefulness and made love, slow and easy but every bit as pleasurable.

15

In the morning, they went down to the station, and when Longarm boarded the train, he hurried to his seat, poked his head out the window, and gave her his farewell kiss.

Nothing, he thought, could be finer.

Chapter 3

The southbound train ride down to Pueblo was uneventful for Longarm, except for the fact that he knew it would be his last in a good long while. Over the years, he'd ridden the Denver and Rio Grande dozens of times, both south as far as Pueblo or north to Cheyenne, where he could connect with the Union Pacific.

"It was good to have you on board again, Marshal," the conductor said as Longarm prepared to disembark. "Got another outlaw to bring back dead or alive?"

"I have two of them waiting for me up at Copper Creek," Longarm replied. "They're a bad pair. I'll be wanting to return them to Denver in your mail car. Is that all right?"

"No problem. Better you confine them in the mail car than out among the passengers. What did this pair do?"

"They're accused of torturing and murdering those postal clerks last year on this very train," Longarm answered.

The conductor, a burly Irishman named Mike Fitzpatrick who was several years past his prime, flushed with anger, then raised his knotted fists. "I wish you'd let me have a piece of 'em before they get turned over to the courts! I'd teach them a thing or two about justice!"

"I know what you mean," Longarm said. "But I'm an officer of the law and I have a sworn duty to protect the accused. Might be they are innocent."

"Humph!" Fitzpatrick scoffed. "I'll bet they're as guilty of sin as Adam."

Longarm saw no point in debating the issue. Over the years, he'd had to learn simply to do his own job and let the courts and judges do theirs. However, there were times when protecting an obviously guilty man tried all of his patience. And more than once, Longarm had wished that his prisoner would attempt something foolish so that putting a bullet in the man would be justifiable. But a real lawman couldn't and wouldn't let his personal feelings interfere with his sworn duty.

"Good luck, Marshal!" the Irishman called when Longarm jumped off the train and landed on the passenger platform in Pueblo. He hurried into town, not bothering to waste four bits on a waiting horse-drawn cab because he was traveling light and fast.

Longarm went straight to Goddard's Livery, passing two of the man's competitors. He had known Bob Goddard for at least ten years, and had never gotten a bad rental horse or uncomfortable saddle from the man. Bob wouldn't have a bad animal on his place, and he kept all his horses well fed and shod.

"Hey, Bob, I need a horse first thing tomorrow morning."

"You rode Duke the last time you were here and he's yours if you want him again," the proprietor offered, hitching up his bib overalls and shoving a piece of chewing tobacco in his mouth. "Duke is a good mountain horse with a lot of stamina."

"He'll do fine," Longarm replied, remembering the tall bay gelding. "And I guess that I'll be renting two more."

Goddard's shaggy eyebrows shot upward. He was an

unkempt man who only bothered to bathe and shave on the first Sunday of each month. "Marshal, are you bringing back prisoners?"

"That's the plan."

"Then maybe you'd prefer to rent a buckboard and a couple of horses instead. I wouldn't charge but an extra dollar a day. Government can afford that, can't they?"

"Sure," Longarm said. "But I'd rather have some distance between myself and my prisoners."

Bob spat a stream of tobacco into the dirt, chewing and nodding slowly. "That makes sense."

"Exactly how far is it to Copper Creek?"

"About twenty miles as the crow flies. But you know it's all uphill into the mountains from here, and the winding road makes it nearer thirty hard miles."

"It would be slow going, I suppose."

"You can count on that." Bob glanced up at the late afternoon sun. "If you left now, you still wouldn't get there until tomorrow morning. Best thing to do is to lay over here and I'll have the three horses all saddled and ready at daybreak."

"Sounds good. You can send the expenses for the horses into Denver tomorrow morning and that way you'll get paid as soon as possible."

"I'll do it. How is life, Marshal?"

"I'm getting married."

Goddard was a confirmed bachelor, but he apparently had no trouble accepting that other men chose to enjoy matrimony, because he grinned, spat, and stuck out his callused, dirty hand. "Congratulations! Who is the lucky girl?"

"Her name is Elizabeth Bonner."

The man blinked. Then his whiskery jaw sagged before he blurted out, "Oh, my Gawd! Are you fixin' to get hitched to Mr. Clyde Bonner's daughter? The one that owns that huge old cattle ranch outside of Denver?"

"That's right."

19

Goddard wiped his hand on his pants and pumped Longarm's hand a second time, bowing slightly and sleeving away the dribble of tobacco juice running into his chin whiskers. "Man, you got to be the luckiest man in Colorado! What a catch. I guess I'll have to start calling you *Mister* Long instead of Marshal Long, huh?"

"You can just call me Custis."

"I'll call you *rich,* that's what I'll do."

Longarm tried to hide his irritation. He was getting damn sick and tired of everyone telling him he was about to become rich as King Solomon. To their way of thinking, it was as if he had won grand prize in some contest and was going to suddenly be taking wheelbarrow loads of cash to the bank every afternoon. Why couldn't people just assume he was marrying Elizabeth because he loved her and would love her just as much even if she were poor?

"I'll see you at first light," Longarm said, not wanting to voice his displeasure as he turned to leave.

"Yes, sir! And if you ever need some good cow ponies, I'd be happy to start collectin' 'em for you, Mr. Long."

"I'll keep the offer in mind," he shouted over his shoulder.

Longarm went to the Frontier Hotel, a longtime favorite, where he was well known and liked. He rented his usual room, washed and combed his hair, then went back downstairs to enjoy a steak. But no sooner had he sat down to order than a man he'd never met before, wearing a threadbare suit and a fake gold stickpin in his necktie, hurried over and introduced himself.

"Mr. Norman Nateldorf is my name and sound investments are my game. May I join you, Mr. Long?"

Before Longarm could think of a way to tactfully inform the tall, fast-talking man that he would prefer to dine alone, Nateldorf pulled up a chair, leaned far forward, and said, "Mr. Long, let me congratulate you on your great good fortune! I'm sure, as a common marshal, you have long suffered danger and privation, and frankly, sir, I am de-

20

lighted that a loyal, hardworking public servant like your-self can finally enjoy a life of ease."

"Who told you that?" Longarm asked, giving the middle-aged man a thorough going-over and not liking what he saw. Nateldorf was obviously a common shyster. He was also very likely a card gambler presently down on his luck who was hoping to take up a new line of business . . . that of finding a sucker and selling him some worthless property or stocks.

"Why, sir, your good fortune is common knowledge," Nateldorf answered, placing his hand on Longarm's fore-arm and giving it a conspiratorial squeeze. "And as a man who has accumulated quite a handsome nest egg of my own, I can appreciate the fact that there are many charla-tans out there who will try to separate you from your new-found wealth. But not Norman Nateldorf. No, sir!"

"Look here, Norman. I am marrying a lovely young woman, not a family fortune. And I can assure you that my—"

"Say no more!" the gambler cried, throwing up his hands and beaming. "I simply want you to know that the cattle market is very, very capricious and that a wise man always *diversifies* his investments."

Here it comes, Longarm thought.

"Mr. Long, you need to invest in a gold mine, and I just happen to have found one that can make you another for-tune."

"Is that right?"

"Why, sure it is! This mine will double our money within two years! No risk. Only rich returns."

"And exactly where is it?"

"Up higher in the mountains, of course. I . . . well, you can understand why I can't divulge its exact location. The truth is, Mr. Long, I have just recently acquired this un-believably rich claim."

"And how did you do that?"

"I had a little luck at poker a few nights ago. Now, I

21

don't usually play the game, but now and then I make an exception and I won this gold mine." He leaned forward and whispered, although there was no one within hearing distance. "But it does need a bit of capital to be fully productive."

"How much capital?"

Nateldorf begin to milk his mustache. His brow furrowed and he made a long, thoughtful face before he said, "Ten thousand dollars would be a good start."

"No, thanks."

"What!"

"You heard me. I'm not interested in a gold mine."

"But sir!"

"Norman," Longarm said with an edge to his voice. "I'm tired and I'm hungry and I've a steak dinner coming. Furthermore, if you don't leave this instant, I'm going to pick you up and toss you out the front door."

"But I'm offering you an equal partnership in a claim that could make us both fabulously rich!"

Longarm reached across the table. He collected Norman Nateldorf's lapels in his fists and shook the man as a terrier would a rat. Shook the con man so hard that his neck snapped back and forth. "Leave!"

Nateldorf staggered backward, then regained both his balance and his composure. Clearing his throat, he said, "I thought you to be a gentleman, but I see that I was mistaken. I thought you to be wise and shrewd enough to see a real opportunity, but again, I was wrong. You will regret your poor behavior and bad judgment, Mr. Long!"

"*Marshal* Long. Good evening, Norman."

Nateldorf stomped his foot with indignation, straightened his lapels, and managed to compose himself. "Perhaps," the man said, lifting his chin and gazing down his long, hooked nose, "you are simply tired and under strain. If so, I forgive your brutish behavior. I will discuss this rich mining investment with you at a more appropriate time."

"Don't bother. I'm still a lawman and I'm here on business."

"Another time. Perhaps even in Denver."

"How about *never.*"

"You're a complete fool!"

Longarm would have leapt for the insulting man, but Nateldorf spun on his heel and strode away.

"Your steak, Marshal?" the waiter interrupted.

Longarm took his seat and nodded as a steaming platter was placed before him. Soon, he forgot all about Norman Nateldorf. After this meal, he would retire to his room and go to sleep early . . . like a family man. No more late-night drinking or playing cards. It was obvious that everyone was beginning to consider him in a different and loftier light, so he might as well live up to their expectations.

He'd do it for Elizabeth.

Just as he was halfway through his dinner, two of his favorite saloon girls, Carrie and Molly, came rushing into the dining room, all excited. They gave Longarm big hugs and kisses, then plopped down at his table, both jabbering.

"Custis, you tall, dirty dog!" Carrie squealed. "I hear that you hit the jackpot! A cattle ranch, fer Chrissakes!"

"Now, wait."

"Why didn't you tell us you had a big move like that up your sleeve . . . or should I say *pants leg*?" Molly chortled. "My goodness, but you finally stuck your big slicky dickey into a gold mine!"

"Now dammit, stop talking like that!" Longarm hissed. "I *love* Elizabeth Bonner."

"And we love *you,*" Carrie said, leaning over and giving him a kiss. "And that's why we are going to take you upstairs and have one last night that you will never forget."

Both women burst out into hilarious laughter, and when Molly reached under the table and pinched Longarm on the pecker, he came to his feet and shouted, "Ladies, I'm going to bed right now . . . alone. So good night!"

Longarm saw shock and disbelief on their painted faces.

But then he saw the corners of their eyes tighten and their red lips twist downward, and knew they were angry. So before they could lash him with their tongues, he was on his way out the door with every intention of going up to his lonely hotel room.

"If you're going to Copper Creek for those two murderers, you're wastin' your time!" Carrie shouted.

Longarm froze in mid-stride and turned back toward the women, who seemed to have every intention of finishing his dinner and wine.

"What do you mean?"

"I mean that some fella just rushed into the Empress Saloon and told us all that one of the pair escaped and the other is due to be hanged tomorrow."

"What about the marshal?"

"Shot the sonofabitch full of holes!" Carrie cried, laughing hysterically. "I guess he deserved it, the fool!"

Molly also chortled with derision. "Custis, this time you're a little too late. Might as well go back to Miss Bonner and tie the knot."

He marched back to his table. "What else can you tell me?"

"Nothing," Carrie said, cutting a big hunk of his steak and jamming it into her mouth. "Mmm, not bad," she said, making a big show of smacking her fat lips. "But I like mine even rarer."

Longarm swore under his breath and headed for the Empress Saloon, where the girls worked. He would find out if this disastrous news was true or not.

Chapter 4

"Dammit," Longarm swore in frustration. "So how did they break out of Marshal Potter's jail!"

"No one knows except Potter, and he's dead," the man from Copper Creek replied. "We were havin' some drinks . . . well, more than some . . . a lot of drinks in the saloon next door when we heard the shooting. Before he died, Marshal Potter managed to wound the one we captured, but the other one got on a horse and went racin' out of town. He emptied a gun back at us and hit Old Man Beeson. Drilled him right through the gizzard! Beeson was as wide as a wagon but he was a good old boy. The crowd like to tore the wounded fella to pieces before they dragged him back into the jail."

"Why didn't they just string him up last night?"

"Well, Marshal, they would have, except that some of the town leaders argued that if they waited until noon tomorrow, they could advertise the event and it would be real good for business."

"Oh, for Gawd sakes," Longarm growled. "Well, they're going to be real unhappy with me when I arrive and take the prisoner into custody."

"You mean you wouldn't let them hang the bastard?" the man asked with astonishment.

"Of course not."

"But he's a killer! Killed Marshal Potter and them two postal fellas on the train. Why would you want to save his neck from bein' stretched?"

"Because I am a sworn officer of the law and necktie parties are illegal unless ordered by a judge."

The man from Copper Creek shook his head and emptied his glass of beer. "Could use another, Marshal."

"Give us both another round," Longarm called out to the bartender as he placed a coin down. "What did you say your name was?"

"Herb. Herb Slater."

"Herb, tell me what happened to the one that got away."

"Not much to say really. He just got away."

"Didn't the townsfolk chase after him?"

"Well," Herb said, "later they did. After they finished beating the shit out of the one they put in jail. And by then, the other was long gone. I hear they formed a posse, but by then most everyone in town was too drunk to ride. I was too, 'cept I had a wagon load of ore to bring down the mountain, which is why I am here right now talking to you and having this beer."

"And that's all you can tell me?"

"Yep," Herb said. "But if you really do try to stop that hangin' tomorrow, they'll maybe kill you, Marshal. Them are some pretty rough boys up in Copper Creek and they don't cotton to outside interference."

"They had better learn that the law is the law."

"Well, sir, no disrespect intended, but you might do well to learn that the people of Copper Creek lost a marshal and a good old boy when them two sonsabitches made their escape. And folks up there ain't gonna be satisfied reading about them fellas being hanged in Denver. No, sir! Honest blood had been spilled, and them rough fellas in

26

Copper Creek ain't of any mind to wait for the wheels of justice to turn at their own slow pace."

Longarm understood, and believed Herb about the vengeful state of mind now present in Copper Creek. Those people would be in a mood to celebrate tomorrow's noontime hanging.

But the law, dammit, was the law.

With his mind made up, Longarm decided that he could not wait until morning to ride to Copper Creek. No, it would be far better to rent two horses instead of the three he'd originally intended, and then head out tonight. He could be in Copper Creek before dawn. Maybe he'd have to sneak the prisoner out in the dark in order to avoid a complete riot. After delivering him to the marshal here in Pueblo, he could then return to Copper Creek and take up the trail of the other murdering sonofabitch before it grew completely cold.

Traveling from Pueblo up to Copper Creek was a difficult and taxing ride that took most of the night. Longarm was dog tired when he finally rode into Copper Creek just before sunrise. He had no trouble locating the marshal's office because most everything else except a saloon was dark and shuttered.

Through the grimy front window of the marshal's office, Longarm could see a crowd. Most were sitting in chairs, all were heavily armed, and from the loudness of their voices, all were very drunk.

This isn't going to be easy, he thought. In fact, this might be damned difficult.

Longarm wrapped the reins of his rental horses loosely around the hitching post and checked his side arm. He wore a double-action Colt .44–.40 on his left hip with the butt turned forward because he preferred a cross-draw. For insurance, he also had a hideout gun. It was a twin-barreled .44-caliber derringer connected to his gold watch chain. That way, someone would think he was just checking his

Ingersol watch instead of bringing out the vicious little pistol. The derringer wasn't worth a damn beyond fifteen or twenty paces, but up close it was a man-stopper, and had saved Longarm's bacon more than once during his many years as a peace officer.

Satisfied that both weapons were ready, Longarm removed his badge from his pocket and pinned it on his coat. If these boys put up an argument or even a fight, he wanted it to be well understood from the start that he was the law and had come to do his duty . . . unpopular though that might be.

"Hello," he said, stepping into the marshal's office to be greeted by a round of dull, bloodshot eyes and empty stares. "I'm here to collect the prisoner."

Longarm glanced at the jail. He could see a man so severely beaten that his face resembled a crushed grape. He was covered with blood, and Longarm figured he ought to be dead.

"Who are you?" a barrel-chested miner demanded, pushing himself to his feet in front of the marshal's desk.

"I'm U.S. Deputy Marshal Custis Long and I've been sent from Denver to bring back that man alive. He'll be tried in a court of law, sentenced, and then almost certainly hanged."

"Well," the miner growled as his equally drunken friends slowly began to understand that there was a serious threat to their necktie party, "we're gonna save the gaw-damn government taxpayers some money and hang that sumbitch ourselves."

"I'm afraid I just can't let you do that."

"Marshal, not you or even a whole passel of lawmen as big as yourself could stop us from hanging that man today at noon," the big miner challenged, thrusting his lantern jaw forward. "You can only get yourself killed."

Longarm knew that there was no time to argue. Talk would serve to inflame this man and his drunken friends. No, the issue had to be settled immediately. With that decision, Longarm drew his Colt and pistol-whipped the miner, who collapsed in an unconscious heap.

"Don't anyone move!" he ordered, yanking a gun from the fallen man's holster. "I am the law and I will not be disobeyed. I have come to take that man to justice. Where is the key to that jail cell?"

"We lost it, ya big bastard!" shouted a pint-sized miner with a pugnacious nature.

Longarm turned one of his pistols on the little man. "Then find it, Shorty!"

"Go to Hell."

Longarm had a bad moment before he happened to see a key lying on Potter's desk. He snatched it up and marched to the jail cell, gun still trained on angry men who were ready to fight him to the death.

"Get up!" Longarm ordered the prisoner. "I'm taking you to Pueblo, then Denver."

The prisoner was barely able to raise his head. By then, Longarm had the cell door open. "Get up, or so help me I'll let them go ahead and hang you!"

Somehow, the prisoner understood and struggled to his feet. He swayed over to Longarm, nearly collapsing in his arms.

"Stand up, dammit!"

The prisoner stood, and they edged past the crowd toward the front door. Longarm felt the anger directed at him. One of the men said, "You'll never get away with this, Marshal. Turn him loose!"

"No."

Longarm backed into the doorway and said to his prisoner, "There are two horses tied to the hitching rail. Mount one."

"I'll do it," the prisoner choked. "I'll do it!"

Longarm did not dare turn and watch as his prisoner swayed over to the horses. He could not risk turning his attention away from the roomful of men for even an instant.

But he did hear the creak of saddle leather and then . . . then he heard the prisoner shout, "Ya!"

Suddenly, his prisoner was whipping his horse in a mad dash to escape. Longarm spun around and fired his Colt in a smooth, unhurried motion. The prisoner raised up in his stirrups and Longarm shot him again, spilling the body from his saddle.

"Gawdamn you, Marshal!" someone choked. "We could have made a lot of money today hangin' that bastard!"

"I'm sorry that I spoiled your necktie party," Longarm replied. "What was his name?"

"George Larson. The one that got away is named Pete Walsh."

"What does he look like?"

"He's about your size with red hair and a scar on his right cheek."

Longarm nodded. "Which way did Walsh leave town?"

"West, higher into the mountains."

"Then that's the way I'm riding and nobody better try to stop me."

There were curses hurled at Longarm as he rode slowly out of Copper Creek. He caught up his extra rental horse, and didn't look back until he topped a ridge and the sun peeked over the eastern horizon.

This is not starting off to be one of my better days. Longarm decided with a yawn.

Chapter 5

Longarm had a name and he had a description that he hoped would soon allow him to capture the deadly killer. But that didn't make him any too happy as he rode higher into the mountains, stopping everyone he met on the road to ask about the fugitive from Copper Creek. Why wasn't he happy? Because he had promised Elizabeth Bonner that this would be a quick and easy assignment. And it should have been, dammit! But now, he might have to hunt Pete Walsh for weeks, thus postponing his own eagerly anticipated wedding. What an aggravation! He should have been firm and refused Billy Vail's request to do this one last assignment.

Elizabeth wouldn't be happy and old Clyde Bonner would be incensed. But there was no help for that now. Longarm knew that he could not, in clear conscience, allow Pete Walsh to simply disappear, probably to kill many more good men. So he was stuck. He'd been too accommodating for a friend, and it was costing him plenty.

Just the thought of being late for his own wedding made Longarm so angry that, in the days that followed, he pushed not only himself but Duke and the other rented horse to their absolute physical limits. And by the time he struggled into the little logging town of Big Pine up near the Continental Divide, he was both hungry and haggard.

"Mister," the liveryman said as Longarm wearily dismounted, "I can't figure out which looks worse—you or your horses."

"Rub them down and grain 'em well," he said. "And I think they need new sets of shoes."

The liveryman raised each animal's forefeet and inspected them carefully. "Their shoes are worn down next to nothing."

Longarm showed the man his badge. "I'm looking for a big redheaded fella with a scar on his right cheek."

"He riding a blaze-faced sorrel with two white stockings?"

"I have no idea."

"Well, if he was, I seen your man. He came through here about . . . four days ago. He was dead broke and looking for work."

"As a logger?"

"As whatever he could find," the liveryman said. "He even asked me for work in exchange for a place to throw his blankets and for boarding his horse. But I didn't like his looks so I sent him down to the freighting company, where I'd heard they were desperate for more mule skinners."

Hope stirred in Longarm's heart. "And which freighting company would that be?"

"The only one in town worth a damn. It's called Ajax Freighting and you can't miss their office on our main street."

Longarm turned and gazed down the main street. There weren't more than a dozen buildings on either side. "I guess I'll ride down there and see what they can tell me."

"You come back and I'll take care of them horses. With bad shoes and the way they're lookin', you won't ride 'em too much farther."

Longarm remounted and rode down to Ajax. It was just

an office that fronted a yard where he saw a lot of huge freight wagons, some of them loaded with logs. After tying up his horse, he sauntered into the office.

"Can I help you?" a middle-aged woman with silver hair and a friendly smile asked from behind a desk.

"My name is Custis Long. I'm a U.S. deputy marshal from Denver and I'm looking for a big redheaded fella. He's got a scar on his right cheek and his name is Pete Walsh. Have you seen him?"

"What's he wanted for?" the woman asked, her smile dying as she jumped to her feet.

"No disrespect, but that's my business, ma'am."

"But you want him for some crime, don't you?"

"Yes, ma'am. And I ought to tell you that he is dangerous."

The woman swallowed hard. "That's what I told my husband when he hired Jeff last week."

"You say the big redheaded fella called himself Jeff?"

"That's right. Jeff Mashburn."

Longarm removed his hat and ran his fingers wearily through his hair. Replacing his hat, he forced a smile and said, "Is Jeff around here now?"

"I wish he were. My name is Loretta Hanson. Me and my husband own this company. We started it six years ago from scratch and with less than a thousand dollars. We've done right well. Ajax Freighting employs four mule skinners in the summertime, but only half that many in winter because of the deep snow."

"What about Jeff Mashburn?"

"He's driving a wagon in from the logging camps located up north. I expect him back here by sundown."

"Tell me where the camp is and I'll go meet him," Longarm decided.

"From the looks of you, Marshal, I'd suggest you bunk down in the back room and wait. Pete or Jeff or whatever his name is strikes me as being a very rough customer. I wouldn't have hired him, but Al said that we can't afford

33

to be choosy in the busy season. And I will admit, the man does know how to handle a team of mules."

Longarm could not stifle a huge yawn. "Maybe I will take you up on your offer, Mrs. Hanson. But first I had best take my horses back to the livery."

"Never mind that. We have plenty of hay and grain. We'll take care of your horses."

"You are very kind."

"To be honest, I just want to get rid of Jeff Mashburn before he kills someone or rob us. We carry a fair amount of cash in our safe. Is he a thief . . . or a killer?"

"Both."

The woman paled slightly. "I'll get a man to take care of your horses. But first, I'll show you the cot we have in the office. You'll be able to sleep there undisturbed."

"I have to be awakened in time to—"

"I know. You don't want to be sawin' logs when Jeff—I mean Pete—shows up on our wagon. Don't fret about a thing. I'll keep a sharp eye out for 'em and give you enough time to wake up proper."

"Thanks again."

"Just don't let the man start shooting and maybe killing someone."

"I'll try not to. Is he packing an iron?"

"Not on his hip, but all our drivers have shotguns or rifles."

Longarm nodded, and allowed the woman to lead him into the back office. He found the cot, thanked her again, and fell asleep almost as soon as his head landed on a dirty old pillow.

When Mrs. Hanson roughly awakened him many hours later, Custis jumped up and reached for his gun.

"Easy!" she said.

"Is Mashburn back?"

"Yes. He just pulled into our freight yard and is starting to unhitch the mules."

"Thanks," Longarm said, climbing to his feet.

"Is there anything my husband or I can do to help?"

"Just stay out of the way. I expect Mashburn or whatever his name is carries a side arm, although it might be hidden."

"He looks real tough. All my other mule skinners step out of his way. I hope you aren't thinking of trying to take him by force."

"No, ma'am."

"Good."

Longarm put on his hat and coat, then headed for the front office with the woman right behind him. A grayhaired man stepped into his path and said, "I'm Al Hanson, Marshal. Can we help you?"

"I don't think so," Longarm replied. "But thanks for the offer."

"I'm not much good with a pistol, but I'm a hell of a fine rifle shot."

"All right," Longarm said, "then back me up if anything goes wrong."

"Should I shoot to kill?"

Longarm took a deep breath. If the redheaded fugitive had only been a stagecoach robber or had committed some lesser crime, the answer would have been no. But since Mashburn was a known killer, Longarm nodded. "Yes. Shoot to kill if he gets me down or kills me."

"I'll do it."

"I'm a good shot too," the man's wife said, grabbing a big double-barreled shotgun from a cabinet and checking the loads. "We'll make sure that Jeff doesn't leave this yard alive."

"Just be real careful not to hit me by mistake," Longarm warned, suddenly concerned for his own safety. "I don't want to be in the middle of a shooting gallery."

"We'll be careful," Mr. Hanson vowed.

Longarm hurried outside, then slowed his pace when he saw his man. Mashburn had a lot of size on him. He was as tall as if not taller than Longarm, and maybe twenty pounds heavier.

Longarm judged him as a very tough customer, and forced himself to smile as he approached the killer, who was yanking a harness off a roan mule.

"Mr. Mashburn?"

"Yeah," the man replied, barely offering him a glance.

Longarm drew his Colt, cocked, and pointed it at the redhead with his right hand while he produced his badge with his left. "I'm U.S. Deputy Marshal Long and you are under arrest. Drop the harness and put your hands over your head!"

Mashburn jumped between the lead mules and they spooked, one slamming sideways into Longarm. When he fired, the mules went crazy and all hell broke loose. Next thing he knew, Longarm found himself on the ground with Mashburn sprinting across the freight yard. One of the mules got tangled in its harness and started kicking furiously. Longarm cried out in pain as a hoof struck him in the right shoulder. His gun went flying, but he rolled and snatched it up in his left hand.

A single rifle shot and the blast of a shotgun caused the mules to go even crazier. Longarm was damned near trampled to death before he could jump up and run over to the killer, who was writhing on the ground and already soaked with blood. Although the light was poor, he could see that the rifle had put a big hole in Mashburn's shoulder. The bullet wound was not fatal by itself, but Mrs. Hanson's shotgun blast had nearly torn the outlaw's leg from his body.

"Get a doctor!" Longarm shouted, knowing that the man would bleed to death in minutes. "Get a rope!"

"You gonna hang him in *that* condition?" Mr. Hanson asked, looking shocked.

Longarm holstered his gun and grabbed at his right shoulder, which hurt like hell from the mule kick. "No," he grated, "I'm going to try and stop the bleeding."

"You can try but you won't," the freight company owner said, standing back and watching Mashburn twist and groan. "Might as well let nature take its course."

"Get a rope or something for me to use as a tourniquet, dammit!"

"Okay, but it's a waste of time," the man replied as his wife stood with a smoking shotgun clenched in her fists.

"I *knew* he would make a fight!" Loretta Hanson declared, keeping the barrel of the shotgun pointed at Mashburn.

"Why don't you go find a doctor!"

"Ain't one in Lone Pine. Let the bastard die. While you was sleeping, we learned what he did to Marshal Potter over in Copper Creek. Potter and Old Man Beeson. He killed 'em both and they were good men."

Longarm knelt beside Mashburn, but he looked up at the woman and said, "That may be true but—"

"Watch out!" she cried.

Too late Longarm glanced down to see the dying fugitive wrench free a Bowie knife from under his jacket. Longarm still had his gun in his fist and he fired point-blank into Mashburn's face just as the fugitive stabbed him in the thigh with the knife.

"Shit!" Longarm cried, falling back and firing again, this time putting one through the dead man's eye.

"Lordy, you should have let me finish him off!" the woman shouted. "Now look what he's done to ya!"

Longarm grabbed the dead man's hand and yanked both it and the knife away. He clamped his own hand over the wound and swore at his own carelessness. His right shoulder was killing him, and he suspected that it was broken.

"Marshal," the woman said, "we better get you inside and take care of that knife wound."

"You have any whiskey?"

"All that you require."

He allowed her to help him to his feet and then he hobbled into the office, where he collapsed in a chair just as

37

the woman's husband and two other men burst inside. "What happened!"

"He had a knife and stabbed me," Longarm hissed between his clenched teeth.

"That sonofabitch was tough!"

"I need whiskey."

But the man wasn't listening. "How'd he find the strength and the will to pull it out when he was in such bad shape?"

"Beats me," Longarm gritted, dragging out his pocketknife with his left hand after discovering his right arm and hand were going numb.

"He was a mean, mean man!" Loretta Hanson said, hurrying into the room with a full bottle of whiskey and a glass.

Longarm didn't waste time pouring. He bit into the cork, spat it away, then took a long pull on the bottle. A moment later, he splashed the liquor on his leg wound, then drank more of it straight.

"Good Gawd almighty," Mrs. Hanson said. "You drink that stuff like it was water."

"Get me some bandages," Longarm said, feeling weak as he clamped his hand back on his thigh. "We need to stop this bleeding now!"

Ten minutes later, Longarm was still sipping from the bottle. His head was spinning, but the wound had stopped bleeding. He was sure that his shoulder was broken and needed to be set or at least supported with a sling. But at least he'd live to return to Elizabeth Bonner, and maybe he'd even get there in time for his own wedding.

Used goods and not in very good condition, but he figured Elizabeth would have him for her husband anyway.

Chapter 6

Dr. Andrew Teal shook his head. "Marshal Long, that shoulder is broken, all right. And I'd say in more than one place. The only thing I can do is put it in a sling. You need to rest and let nature take its full course. I'd say it will be healed nicely in another . . . oh, three or four months. Is the government going to give you that much time off?"

"I'm resigning. What about the knife wound?"

"It was deep but it is healing nicely. You were very fortunate that it didn't sever an artery. I'm sure it's sore."

"Damn right."

"So that's it," the doctor mused. "I'd like you to come by tomorrow afternoon and I'll—"

"Doc, I'll be on the Denver and Rio Grande tomorrow. How much do I owe you?"

The physician shook his head. "No charge."

"Why not?"

"I knew Marshal Potter. He was a good man. I also heard about the others that were murdered by that pair. You are to be congratulated."

"Thanks," Longarm said, struggling back into his shirt. "But the truth is, I didn't kill either one of the murderers."

"So I heard. Mr. and Mrs. Hanson have become celebrities up in Big Pine, and the town of Copper Creek is still celebrating."

"Those Copper Creek boys don't need much of a reason to celebrate," Longarm said morosely. "But thanks for your help and for not charging anything."

"My pleasure. You just need time to recover. The numbness in your right arm and hand will gradually disappear. You say your fingers are tingling?"

"Yes."

"Wiggle them for me."

Longarm did as he was told.

"No problem," the doctor assured him. "You'll make a complete recovery."

"You're sure of that?"

"Very. You need to understand that there was some nerve damage up in your shoulder. From what I can tell, it's a nasty fracture. Probably multiple fractures. And you may find you have some lasting pain. It might get worse as you get older, and cold winter weather will not improve the situation."

"And there's nothing to be done?"

"Move to Arizona and it would definitely feel better in their dry heat."

"I got other plans," Longarm said, thinking of Elizabeth and his upcoming wedding.

"I'm glad to hear that," Dr. Teal said. "From the looks of you, I'd say it was time to find another line of work. A safer, more comfortable one."

Longarm nodded in agreement. He was still questioning his own abilities after losing both fugitives. Billy Vail had ordered him to bring them back alive, and he'd failed his friend twice.

It was time to turn in his badge.

Because of Longarm's broken shoulder and the constant jostling movement of the train, the trip back to Denver

40

was an unremitting agony. Longarm was limping badly, and his physical appearance was quite shocking. He seemed to have aged a year in less than one week, shocking the conductor and other train employees who knew him well.

"Custis!"

Longarm turned to see Billy Vail hurrying through the crowd at the Denver station. He'd telegraphed the man to inform him of what had taken place in Copper Creek and Big Pine. And now, Billy looked visibly upset.

"Custis, I'm sorry for sending you down there," Billy blurted out. "I . . . I can't tell you how bad I feel."

"It's not your fault," Longarm answered. "Everything that could go wrong for me did go wrong. It leaves no doubt in my mind that this is the time for me to hand in my badge."

He looked around at the crowd. "I sort of hoped that Elizabeth might come to meet me. I sent a telegram, but . . ."

Billy paled. "I have some terrible news, Custis."

"Is she sick!" he asked with alarm.

"Elizabeth . . . is dead."

Longarm went as crazy as the mules up in Big Pine. One minute he was balanced on his good leg; the next he was screaming and cursing. He even tried to smash Billy Vail with his hand.

"I'm sorry," Billy kept repeating.

When Longarm finally calmed down, Billy explained. "Someone murdered Elizabeth and her father. The boy was hiding and we don't know if he witnessed the murders or not. He's still in shock. I've got every available officer at the ranch investigating, and it looks to us like a pure case of robbery. They forced Clyde Bonner to open his safe. Then they killed him anyway."

Longarm started hobbling toward the waiting cab. He wanted to be at Elizabeth's side and . . .

"We buried them yesterday," Billy said, jumping in

front of his friend. "Custis, they were murdered just two days after you left for Pueblo."

He swung around. "Why didn't you contact me!"

"We tried," Billy told him. "God knows I tried. We just couldn't locate you. Come on, I'll take you to my house. You need sleep. And I know that words don't mean a thing at a time like this, but I swear to you on my mother's grave that we will find out who murdered Elizabeth and her father. We'll find them if we have to go to the ends of the earth. They won't get away with it, Custis. I swear. . . ."

Longarm took a ragged breath. He hadn't cried since he was a small boy, but now he scraped unbidden tears away with the back of his hand. "You said 'they.' How do you know there was more than one?"

"Tracks. Evidence. We think there were at least four intruders. Maybe five. If the boy will start talking, I'm sure that he can confirm those numbers. Someone who was headed out to the ranch said they saw four riders galloping hard toward the mountains."

"Where the hell were all the cowboys!" Longarm demanded with exasperation. "And the maid and . . ."

"The entire household staff was executed," Billy said, spitting out his words like bitter seeds. "We found them bound and shot. The animals who did this were a pack of cold-blooded sonofabitches who eliminated all the witnesses. They'd have killed the boy too if they knew he was in the house."

Longarm's head slumped forward and he squeezed his eyes shut. "I'm going out there."

"Custis, there's no use in doing that. At least not for a few days. Man, you are out on your feet and look like death."

"I'm going," Longarm whispered, head snapping up. "So the only question I have is, are you going with me?"

"Of course."

"Then let's not say another thing. Let's just get a buckboard or a carriage and head for the Bonner Ranch!"

"Anything you say," Billy answered. "I've got our best men working on the case. Jim Talbot. Charlie West. Abe Sinclair. You know they are the best and they'll never quit. And neither will I. I swear. . . ."

"Billy?"

"Yeah?"

"Shut the hell up."

Billy Vail wasn't used to being talked to that way, but he closed his mouth as they headed for a waiting cab.

When Longarm arrived at the murder scene, he went over it very carefully with the investigators, all of whom were his respected colleagues. He'd ridden with these men and he'd fought with them and helped break important cases. They were his friends, but they'd followed a trail that had already run cold in the mountains, and now they had few leads to follow and no names or faces to help them to catch the four thieves and murderers.

"Well," he said to them all as they stood in the huge living room where he and Elizabeth had spent so many happy hours together, "it seems to me that the boy is the key to finding out who murdered Elizabeth and her father. Where is he?"

"Josh is in Denver staying with his mother's aunt. He is under the watchful eye of a doctor and heavily medicated. The boy seems to have gone into sort of a trance. He doesn't talk and acts as if he doesn't hear. The doctor says that he needs to see a specialist and might have suffered some kind of irreparable brain damage."

"I know Josh better than anyone . . . including a doctor," Longarm said. "I'll talk with him."

"I'm not sure the doctor will allow that," Billy said carefully.

"And why not?"

"He might think that your presence would be too powerful a reminder of what Josh lost in the death of his mother. Custis, you can't bring back Elizabeth or the others that died here, and further damaging the boy by trying to force him to remember this horror might be a terrible mistake."

"But we have to know if he *saw* the killers!"

Billy shrugged. "Why don't you talk to the doctor in charge of Josh's care and recovery? His name is Milton Silverman and he has an excellent reputation as a specialist in mental disorders."

"I'll do that today."

"Shall we head back to Denver?" Charlie West asked.

"You go ahead," Longarm told them. "I'll be along directly."

"Sure," Billy said. "Take your time."

Longarm walked out to visit the fresh graves. Besides that of Elizabeth and her father, there were three others. He removed his hat and sat down on his haunches beside Elizabeth's grave, then placed his hand on the freshly exposed soil and whispered, "I'm deeply sorry. If I had listened to you and not gone south, this might not have happened. I will never forgive myself for being absent when you most needed me."

Longarm took a ragged breath and continued. "But I swear that I'll kill them all. I'll hunt them down, then shoot them in the guts so they die screaming. I won't let them die quick or easy."

Longarm ran his fingers over the smooth mound of the grave. "And I'll come back and make sure that everything on earth is done to help your son. I'll get him to the best specialist in the world. I'll be a father to him like we always talked about . . . if he wants. I'll devote my life to making up for this, Elizabeth!"

He sat there beside her grave for nearly an hour, talking and making promises. And finally, when one of the waiting horses whinnied, he roused out of his hate-filled reverie and went to join the others, announcing a decision that he knew would not be popular.

"Billy," Longarm said, offering the marshal his badge, "I'm resigning as of right now."

Billy retreated. "Give yourself at least a few weeks before you do something you might come to regret. You're not in any shape to make this decision. Besides, I'd sort of thought that you . . ."

"What?" Longarm asked when it became clear that Billy was at a complete loss for words.

"That you'd want to be in charge of this investigation. That you'd insist on being the principal investigator and the one that tracks down the killers, arrests them, and brings them to trial."

"No trial," Longarm said in a cold, hard voice. "I'm going to turn bounty hunter."

"What!" Billy's shock was reflected in the faces of the other lawmen.

"You heard me," Longarm told them all. "The killers of this family and its staff will have a bounty placed on their heads, won't they?"

"Of course! And a huge one."

"Then I mean to collect and give it to Josh."

Billy shook his head back and forth. "Custis, you know that boy will never want for money. He'll inherit this ranch."

"Then I'll distribute the bounty to the relatives of the murdered household staff," Longarm decided out loud. "But what you boys all need to understand is that I don't want any help . . . or interference . . . not even from you people who are my well-meaning friends."

"Now wait a minute here!" Billy protested. "This is—"

"*Personal.*"

"Custis, it sounds to me like you plan to take the law into your own hands," Charlie West said. "That you mean to catch and kill these men."

"Then it sounds right, Charlie."

"Now hold on," Billy shouted. "You can't just take the law into your own hands!"

"I can and I will. This is going to get bloody, so you'd better make it plain that the reward for the men who murdered Elizabeth Bonner and the others reads alive . . . or *dead.*"

Abe Sinclair and Jim Talbot nodded in agreement. Charlie West said, "I'm not going to interfere on this one."

"You will if I tell you to!" Billy stormed.

"No, sir, I will not," Charlie said, folding his arms across his chest.

"Me neither," Abe added.

"Nor me, sir," Jim Talbot said, turning to speak directly to Longarm. "Custis, the men who did this don't deserve any justice. They don't deserve the quick, clean death they'd receive by dropping through the floor of a gallows either. What they deserve is to die slow."

"I just made a promise to Elizabeth that they'd die screaming . . . and they will."

But Billy had other ideas. "Elizabeth was a gentlewoman, and I don't believe she would sanction what you have in mind."

"Billy, you only met my fiancée once or twice. So don't tell me what she would want. Just let this one go."

"I can't," he said. "The governor will be on my ass day and night until this case is solved."

"Then tell him it will be."

"By a man so filled with hate he admits that this will be a bloody vendetta?"

"You can say that . . . or say nothing. Makes no difference to me."

"Custis, if you find and execute those men, you'll be no better than they are."

"I disagree," he said, turning to leave. "And now I'm going to see Josh, and God help you or anyone else who tries to get in my way."

"He means it, Boss," Jim Talbot said. "You got no choice but to let him do what has to be done."

"I know," Billy replied. "And, if you think it's those

four killers I'm worried about, think again. I'm just afraid that Custis Long, as we've known him, will never be the same."

The three deputy marshals solemnly nodded their heads in understanding.

Chapter 7

"What the hell are these newspaper people doing out here in the street?" Longarm snarled when they arrived to see Josh.

Billy Vail frowned. "This case has caused quite a sensation."

"Excuse me," a young man with a notepad in his hand called, racing up to intercept Longarm and Billy as they started to open the picket-fence gate and go up to the house. "Can I have a few words with you about the Bonner kid?"

"No," Longarm snapped.

"Who are *you*?"

"Never mind that," Billy said, trying to push the over-zealous reporter out of the way. "Just let us pass."

"Can you at least tell us if the boy saw who murdered his mother and grandfather? What's the state of the investigation and what was the motive?"

"I'm afraid we don't have any answers yet."

"How did the kid survive?"

"He hid in his bedroom upstairs," Billy said, trying to open the gate in order to get past the reporter.

"Is he a witness? Can he identify the murderers?"

"He's not talking."

"Why not? Is he addled?"

Longarm grabbed the reporter with his left hand and shoved him so hard, the man tripped and fell over backward. This caused a near-riot among the other reporters, and the scene was bedlam. It took all of Longarm's reserve not to wade into the bunch of them swinging.

"Insensitive bastards," Billy muttered as they finally got through the gate and headed up the walk to the house.

When Longarm and Billy reached the front door, a policeman asked them their names before they were allowed to pass inside.

"You had better tell those reporters that when I come out, I'm going to be bashing some skulls if they don't back away from me," Longarm warned the policeman.

"I'll do the best that I can," he replied. "But that's a public street out there and they got a right to stand in it."

Longarm was in no mood to debate the issue. He swept off his hat when he saw Nellie Bass and said, "I got here just as soon as I could, Nellie. How is Josh?"

Josh's aunt was only about five feet tall, but she was pert and spunky. However, when she saw Longarm, tears spilled from her eyes. Nellie hurried across the room and they embraced. "I kept prayin' you'd get here soon. Josh is in shock. I don't know what to think and neither does Dr. Silverman."

"Is he eating and sleeping?"

"Not much."

"Talking?"

"Just a few words like 'yes' or 'no.' Custis, it's as if he has blocked everything from his mind. He stares at the wall and cries a lot. Maybe you can do something for him."

"I'm here to try. Nellie, this is my good friend, Billy Vail. I worked for him quite a few years and he is heading up the murder investigation."

"Any leads?"

49

"None, I'm afraid," said Vail. "We tracked the suspects north and then west into the mountains, but it rained so hard we lost the tracks. No one up there has reported seeing four strangers. Word of the killings and a plea to help us solve the case has been telegraphed to every law officer within five hundred miles. But we just don't have descriptions, so we're in trouble."

Nettie turned to look up at Longarm. "You will find and bring them back to be hanged, won't you?"

"If it takes the rest of my life."

"You look terrible. What happened to your arm and your leg?"

"It doesn't matter."

"It does to me. Now what happened?"

"I got kicked by a mule in the shoulder. It's broken, but healing fine. As for my leg, I got stabbed."

"Oh, dear!"

"It'll pass, Nellie. What matters now is Josh and capturing his mother's killers." Longarm motioned toward a closed door. "Is the boy in that bedroom sleeping?"

"Yes."

"I need to see him now."

Nellie grew agitated. "I'm not sure that's such a good idea."

"Why not?"

"Because Dr. Silverman said that he was the only one that should ever bring up the subject of murder. He's afraid that if the memories are revived before he's strong enough to handle them, Josh could have a complete mental breakdown . . . perhaps even go insane!"

"Custis," Billy said, "you feel guilty enough already, and you'd never forgive yourself if you further harmed the boy."

"I know. But he's the only one that can help us find those killers. If he doesn't give us something to go on, we're licked before we begin."

"But . . ."

"I'll talk to him about *other* things."

"He may not utter a single word," Nellie warned.

"I'm prepared for that."

"All right, talk to him," Nellie reluctantly agreed as she nervously wrung her hands together. "Mr. Vail, would you like something to drink?"

"Such as?"

"Tea or rye whiskey. That's all I have in the house other than water."

"The rye whiskey would be welcomed."

"In that case, I believe I'll have a glass myself."

When Longarm entered the small bedroom, Josh Bonner was lying on the bed, hands folded across his chest. He was a lanky boy, tall for his age, with sandy hair and brown eyes. Longarm genuinely liked Josh, and had looked forward to being his stepfather. Now, that dream was as dead as his lovely mother.

"Josh, how are you?"

The boy didn't even turn his head to look at Custis.

"Maybe I'm so beat up you don't recognize me," Longarm went on.

"You're Custis."

"That's right. My shoulder got broken by a damn mule. He kicked and stomped me pretty good. And this leg wound," he said, pointing downward. "Well, I got careless and a dying murderer stabbed me when I turned my head for a minute."

Josh gave him no response.

Longarm sat on the edge of the bed. "I wasn't there for you and your family and I'm sorry," he said as his voice thickened with emotion. "I was wrong to take another assignment. If I'd stayed around, your mother, grandfather, and those others in the house might still be alive. Can you forgive me?"

The boy finally turned to him. "It wasn't your fault."

"Nellie says you're not talking. Why?"

51

"I got nothing to tell anybody," Josh said, his lower lip starting to tremble.

"Maybe you can tell me who the killers are," Longarm said calmly. "I can't bring back your mother or the rest, but I want to find those men."

"You'd only arrest them."

"No, I'd kill them slow."

The boy stared at Longarm. "You'd *kill* them?"

"I'd kill them slow. God forgive me, but that's what I'd do."

Tears rolled down Josh's cheeks. "I didn't see them clearly. They came early in the morning and I was still asleep. I was awakened by the sound of screaming. I jumped out of bed and heard gunshots. I didn't have a gun. I tried to think of what to do and I . . . I don't know. I just couldn't move. I was so scared I wanted to hide under the bed, but it was like my feet were nailed to the floor. And the gunshots went on and on. I am such a coward!"

Longarm put his arm around Josh. "You couldn't have saved anyone, and the men robbing your grandfather would have killed you without hesitation. Even with a gun, you wouldn't have stood a chance."

"Maybe I would have, with six bullets and four men of 'em!"

"No. There was nothing you could do to change anything. But you can do something now and that's to help me find them."

"I told you that I didn't really see them."

Longarm held him for a while, and then he eased the boy back down on the bed. "Listen to me. There are times in every man's life when they become too scared to do anything. I've been that way before. Even your grandpa has lost his nerve a few times and been filled with shame."

"You don't know that."

"I know every man has had moments in his life when he discovers he isn't quite as tough, brave, or strong as he'd thought himself. But a man gets past that and learns

52

his limits. Fear isn't all bad. Sometimes it saves your life. Men without a normal fear are fools who die young. Brave men face their fears and learn how to deal with them in the face of long odds."

"You'd have gone down there and saved Mother. You've never been afraid of anybody!"

"Not true. When I was a boy I was always afraid of my father. He beat me pretty regularly. He got mean when he was drinking, and he'd whip me until I bled more times than I can recall. I used to piss my britches when he got a whip and chased after me. I'd be so scared I couldn't even run. So I'd just stand there and get whipped."

Josh's eyes widened. "Your own father did that to you?"

"Yes." Longarm took a deep breath. "And you know what?"

"What?"

"When I went to war I had such a hatred built up for that old man that I think it kept me alive. I vowed that I'd survive all the bloody battles and go back to whip my father just the way he'd always whipped me."

"Did you?"

"No," Longarm told him. "The ornery old bastard died before I got back to West Virginia. Momma was long gone to her eternal rest. Pa had broken her spirit and she died in misery. So when I did get home and found Pa resting beside my dear mother, well, I took a sledgehammer and I busted his headstone into a thousand pieces. Then, I pissed all over his grave."

"You did!"

"I did," Longarm admitted. "I never told that to anyone before, so don't you tell it to anyone either. Okay?"

"Sure. But if I came with you and we found my mother's murderers and killed them, I'd piss on their dead bodies!"

"I'd join you," Longarm confessed. "I damn sure would."

"Could I go to help you find them?"

"No."

"Why not?"

"I expect the trail to be long and dangerous."

"But maybe I could help."

"Maybe, but most likely you'd put such a worry on my mind that we'd both get killed. Can you understand how I'd be worrying about you so much that I might get careless?"

"I guess so."

"Josh, tell me everything you heard or saw that morning at the ranch. Don't leave out anything."

The boy lay back down and closed his eyes. "My bedroom door was closed tight and you know the doors in that house are solid oak."

"I know."

"So I didn't hear much of anything."

"That's probably just as well."

"Just some screams and then shots. But . . ."

Longarm leaned closer. "But what?"

"I did see them run out of the house. Their horses were tied up in front, and I watched them mount up from my upstairs window. I watched as they loaded their saddlebags with money and jewelry and raced away."

"You must have seen a little of their faces."

"No, just their backs, because I was looking down and they all wore hats. But three of them did have beards."

"What color?"

"Dark."

"Were they tall or short? Fat or thin?"

"All of them were average-sized, I think."

"That doesn't help me. Can you describe what they were wearing?"

"Just ordinary working clothes."

Longarm smothered his disappointment and asked, "The kind that cowboys wear?"

Josh shook his head. "They weren't cowboys."

"How do you know that?"

54

"I could just tell. Two of them wore black derbies and one . . . one wore a funny little hat."

"Like a cap?"

"Yes!" Josh sat up straighter. "It was a cap."

"What color?"

He closed his eyes for a moment, then said, "Checkered green and red."

"Maybe like a Scottish cap?"

"I guess so. I remember the thing had a brass or silver button on the top. I was looking down and the button glinted in the bright morning sun. And that same man wore a red scarf."

"A long one?"

"Longer than normal. Almost like a shawl. I remember standing there shaking so hard my knees were knocking, but thinking that the scarf was odd. And it matched the red of the man's hat."

"Are you sure?"

"Yes. That one was doing most of the yelling and giving the orders. The others weren't saying anything back, so I guess he was their leader."

"He sounds like a Scot. Did any of them wear chaps or boots?"

"No, but one had a hide vest with hair."

"What color?"

"Black and white. It was kind of fancy and looked to be cut out of a dairy cow."

"Good! Anything else?"

"No."

Longarm was encouraged. "You might remember more tomorrow."

"I don't think so. I've been going over that in my mind again and again. Oh, and the man with the cap on had a short-barreled shotgun. It was cut real short. Custis, please take me with you!"

"Josh, I just can't. Your mother is in heaven, but if she's looking down on us, she's also begging me to do this alone. You're all that she left this world and I won't jeopardize that for anything."

"I won't stay here!" Josh said, exploding in anger. "I'll . . . I'll follow you no matter what."

"Listen. I've got enough to worry about without you. So do me a big favor and stay here with your aunt Nellie."

"When you kill them, will you promise to let me know right away? You could send a telegram, couldn't you?"

"Yes, and I will."

"Promise?"

"You've my word on it," Longarm vowed.

"All right then, I'll stay with Aunt Nellie. But I don't like Dr. Silverman."

"I'll talk to him in the morning."

"He wants to know all sorts of things about Mother and my real father. Even about you and Grandpa. Things that are none of his business."

"I'll tell him to stay away from you until I get back and we talk this over again."

"Maybe he won't do that if you're gone."

"I'll make sure that he understands. I'll make sure that your aunt does as well."

"Okay."

"But I want you to start talking to her," Longarm said. "She's afraid that you've lost your mind."

"I did for a while. Will you come back to me?"

"Count on it."

Josh took Longarm's hand in his own and closed his eyes. "I'd like to sleep for a while now," he said. "I'd like to be quiet."

"Okay."

Longarm smoothed the boy's hair, then got up and limped outside.

"Well?" Nellie asked, looking drawn with anxiety.

"He's going to be all right."

"Did he tell you anything we can use?" Billy asked.

Longarm hated to do it, but he looked at his former boss

and friend and said, "Not a single thing, I'm afraid."

"Damn!"

Longarm removed his Stetson and stretched out on Nellie's horsehair sofa. His shoulder and leg were killing him and he was exhausted.

"Custis, can you eat now?" Nellie asked, hovering over him.

He cocked one eye open and said, "Thanks, Nellie, but I'd rather sleep until tomorrow morning."

She went away, probably in search of a pillow and a blanket.

"Custis?"

He opened his eyes to look up at Billy. "You were in there a long time. The boy *must* have told you something."

"He told me he was so afraid that he pissed in his pants and couldn't go downstairs to help his mother and the others. I tried to tell him that we all know fear one time or another."

"But what about the descriptions?"

"His mind is still a blank."

"Damn!"

"Maybe in time it will come back to him," Longarm said, "but not for a while."

"Then we're stumped. We've got nothing."

"I'm afraid so," Longarm said, with no intention of sharing what he'd learned so that others could join the manhunt. "Sorry."

"Not your fault," Billy told him. "But the kid started talking. That's a good sign. A real good sign. Maybe Dr. Silverman can get something useful out of him about those four killers."

"Josh hates the man. He doesn't want to see him anymore."

"But he needs to!"

"No, he doesn't," Longarm said. "At least not until he says he does."

"So you're going to tell him to stay away from Josh?"

"I'm going to *order* him to stay away from the boy until I return."

"From what! Without descriptions, you've nothing to hunt."

Longarm closed his eyes again. "I'll find them."

"And kill them."

"Billy," Longarm said, "it's time for you to go home to your wife and kids and leave us alone."

"Damn you, Custis! I think you're holding out on me. And, if you are, I'll have you tossed into a federal jail and held without bail."

Longarm's eyes snapped open. "That would be a terrible mistake. Don't do it."

Billy's anger quickly washed away. "All right, I won't. But you've never lied to me before and it hurts."

"I'm sorry."

"So am I," Billy told him as he put his hat on and headed outside.

Chapter 8

Longarm awoke to a loud pounding on Nellie's front door.

"Coming. Coming!" the old woman called as she hurried across the room. "Custis, this will be Dr. Silverman."

"I'll speak to him," Longarm said, knuckling sleep from his eyes and sitting upright on the sofa. "Tell him to wait out on the front porch."

"He won't like that."

"Tell him anyway."

Longarm ran his fingers through his long, unwashed hair. He rubbed his jaw and felt the heavy growth of beard, and brushed at his vest knowing he was filthy and looked completely disreputable. He heard Nellie's voice rising to be heard above that of the physician, who was already upset and yelling.

"Hang on!" Longarm called, pushing to his feet and then limping to the rescue. "Dr. Silverman?"

"Of course. Who are you?"

"Custis Long. I was going to marry the boy's mother."

"Yes. Yes. Well, now you can't marry Miss Bonner. What is the meaning of this outrage? I told this woman that I did not want the boy to be upset or spoken to without my consent. Now, I learn that you have—"

"He won't be seeing you anymore," Longarm said bluntly. "Dr. Silverman, you can leave now and don't come back . . . ever."

"I will do no such thing!"

Silverman was a large man in his forties, soft-looking, with mussed hair, a rumpled suit, red suspenders, and wire-rimmed glasses. He looked intelligent and bookish. He was also arrogant and obviously unaccustomed to taking orders.

"You'll leave now or I'll feed you your teeth," Longarm warned, balling his good left fist.

"You can't do this! You're not even a relative."

"I'm still Josh Bonner's best friend," Longarm said. "And he doesn't like you. In fact, he told me last night that he *hates* you."

"The boy is traumatized and his pain has caused him to be twisted with hatred! What else could we expect after the horror he has suffered? His hatred and inability to deal with the reality concerning the murder of his family is exactly the reason why it is so important that Josh be treated by a professional dealing in mental disorders."

"He says you are asking him questions that have nothing to do with the murders."

"Of course I am. It is critical that I regress him into infancy."

"Hogwash!"

Silverman's bushy eyebrows shot up. "Why, you're nothing but a lawman. I doubt you have much education, and you can't possibly understand what that boy needs. You're only here because you want something from him. What? A share in the Bonner fortune perhaps?"

"Mister," Longarm grated, "I have heard just about enough from you. If you value your health, you'll leave right now."

"I won't be bullied or intimidated. And from the looks of you, I'd say that fisticuffs is the *last* thing you need."

"But it is what you are about to get."

"Listen to me. Without professional help, the boy's hatred will be locked inside, as malignant and poisonous as any cancer. If that happens, I predict that Josh will eventually go crazy or himself become a murderer. Do you hear me? I know what I am talking about, but you know nothing."

Longarm could have punched Silverman in the nose, but instead he just grabbed the physician by the throat and heaved him backward off the porch. The doctor landed in Nellie's rose garden and howled. He jumped up cursing and ran for the gate. Longarm let him go.

"Well," Nellie said, bursting outside again in time to see the physician running down the street, "I don't think he'll ever return."

"He was a pompous ass," Longarm said. "He would have messed with Josh's mind until the kid didn't know whether he was going or coming. Josh is far better off without the man."

"Are you sure?"

"Yes." Longarm leaned back against the door frame. "He'll be talking to you much more now."

"How do you know that?"

"Because I asked him to and he agreed. Josh is going to be all right, but it will take time."

"I heard you tell your friend last night that he couldn't help with descriptions. Is that the truth?"

"No."

Nellie's eyebrows shot up in question. "Am I to understand that you lied to a federal marshal who was also your friend?"

"I did," Longarm admitted. "I'm not proud of the fact."

"Then . . ."

"If Billy had descriptions, he'd have every lawman in Colorado chasing after those four killers. The result would be the gang would spook and scatter so that we'd never find them. I believe the only hope of capturing those four is to have them believe they got away without a single witness. If they think there is no danger, they might get careless, and when they do, I'll be there."

"With a broken shoulder and bad leg?"

"That's right."

"You're taking a big gamble on this theory of yours, aren't you?"

"I suppose so. But all I need to do is find just one of them. If I can take him alive, I'll make him talk and then I'll draw a bead on the others."

"That makes sense."

"Nellie, did you go out to the ranch and look around?"

"Heavens, no!"

"I want you to do that with me today. We'll take Josh with us."

The woman recoiled. "Now wait a minute! That's too much to ask of that boy and I don't see—"

"Maybe they took some things of value downstairs that only you or Josh would miss. Some silver perhaps. It would be likely, and the stolen goods would give me a lead."

"How?"

"I would start with the pawnshops." Longarm sighed. "Nellie, I'm just trying to get a toehold on this case. I'm just looking for a little crack that I can break open. Billy and his men are of the opinion that the killers rode off and are probably hundred of miles away. But I wonder why they'd leave their own territory if they were sure that they were not in any danger of being identified."

"I see what you mean."

"How much money did Mr. Bonner keep in his safe?"

"I have no idea."

"Would he have kept cash?"

"Oh, certainly! He liked to pay his men in cash on the last day of every month."

"And he was killed on the twenty-eighth," Longarm said. "So he probably had his payroll in that safe."

"Why . . . yes, I believe he would have."

"So who would know that other than his cowboys?"

"Everyone in Denver," Nellie said. "The cowboys would come into town and blow off some steam with their pay. It was common knowledge that Clyde paid cash at the month's end."

"I see. Will you come out to the ranch with me?"

"Of course, but I'm concerned about Josh . . . say, Custis!"

"What?"

"Clyde wore a big diamond ring on his left hand. It was made of heavy gold and the diamonds formed a horseshoe. Remember?"

"Sure!"

"I have the personal belongings that were taken from the bodies and that ring wasn't included. Neither was the . . ."

"Diamond engagement ring I gave to Elizabeth?" Longarm choked out.

"That's right!"

"What else?"

"I don't know," Nellie replied. "But Clyde did carry a silver money clip."

"Yes, I saw it. Anything else?"

"Not that I can think of."

Longarm nodded. "All right. We have several items that I can search for in the Denver pawnshops. Even if I don't find them, I might happen to see one of the rings on someone else's finger."

"I suspect," Nellie said quietly, "that finding Elizabeth's ring on another woman's hand or even in a pawnshop would be extremely hard on you."

"Nellie," Longarm said, "there is nothing that can touch the pain I already feel inside. Absolutely nothing. Now let's get Josh and go out there."

Nellie glanced out at the street. "What about the reporters still hanging around? There's not as many as last week, but I see two still waiting."

"We'll go out the back of the house and down the alley. They'll never see us."

"But if they do?"

"I'll convince them to leave us alone," Longarm said.

"Like with Dr. Silverman?"

"If necessary."

They arrived at the Bonner Ranch in a rented carriage at about two o'clock in the afternoon. Josh was pale but alert, and after visiting the graves of his mother and grandfather, the boy seemed stronger and more determined than before to do whatever was necessary in order to help Longarm find the killers.

"Are you sure you're up to going into the house?" Longarm asked as the ranch's cowboys stood at a respectful distance and watched.

"I have to sooner or later," Josh said in a barely audible voice.

Even Nellie was pale and somber as they climbed the familiar front-porch steps and went inside the huge house. The living room where everyone had died had been thoroughly cleaned, the overturned furniture put back in place, and all signs of the carnage erased. Even to Longarm's trained eye, the place seemed quite normal.

"Just look around for a few minutes," Longarm instructed the pair, "and try to determine if anything valuable is missing."

It took less than thirty seconds for Josh to cry out with excitement, "They took the bronze sculpture of Grandpa's first longhorn bull!"

"Are you sure?"

"Yes. His name was Diablo. Don't you remember it?"

"I sure do," Nellie said. "That longhorn sculpture was about eighteen inches tall and quite magnificent. It was the centerpiece of that big wagon-wheel table. Its base was solid silver and I'll bet that was why they took Diablo."

"Anything else?"

"Don't rush us," Nellie sternly answered as she began to prowl the room like a veteran Pinkerton detective.

"The silver chalice that Grandma loved is also gone," Nellie soon announced, staring at a cabinet of blue china dishes. "And . . . and so is all of the beautiful silverware. Each piece is engraved with the letters CB. I remember that Clyde went to Chicago and bought it from a very famous silversmith about three years ago."

"A complete set?" Longarm asked with surprise.

"Yes," Nellie said in a voice that left no doubt of the fact. "A silver service for twenty that cost Clyde a small fortune. Why, it must have weighed a ton!"

"Josh, do you remember seeing those four men haul out sacks of loot?"

"No," the boy admitted, "but they could have done it before I looked down on them. They had the time, and I do seem to recall big gunnysacks tied to their saddle horns."

"A major mistake on their part," Longarm growled. "Good work. Now both of you keep looking."

"You were here too," Josh said.

"I know, but mostly with Mr. Bonner in his library."

Longarm went directly to that book-lined room where he and the old man had spent a considerable amount of time sipping cognac or brandy and smoking as they discussed the business of handling cowboys and profitably raising livestock. Longarm had savored those long, leisurely talks, and during them he'd felt extremely close to the prosperous old cattleman. Clyde Bonner had been a pioneer, and he'd loved to tell stories of his early ranching days.

One thing that Longarm noticed missing was a pair of handsome English dueling pistols. The rare eighteenth-century weapons had been quite a conversation piece, and were worth thousands of dollars. Longarm remembered that Mr. Bonner had proudly displayed them in their original wooden and felt-lined boxes, and had bragged that they could still be fired and with considerable accuracy.

Engraved silverware. Rare dueling pistols. A silver chalice and a longhorn bull named Diablo dancing on silver. Could the four murderers have transported those eyecatching treasures on horseback very far without attracting attention and curiosity? I don't think so. That means that they would be sold as quickly as possible either in Denver or maybe in Cheyenne. But as for Mr. Bonner's horseshoe-shaped diamond ring and money clip, well, that Scot might have kept them . . . if he was very confident and cocky. That and, of course, the cash, which could well have been in the thousands of dollars.

"Josh went outside," Nellie said, breaking Longarm's reverie. "And I think I'm about to do the same."

"Nothing more is missing?"

"There may be a lot more," Nellie replied. "I didn't come to visit all that often because I preferred to live in town where I have many friends."

"What is going to happen to the ranch?" Longarm asked.

"We haven't even talked about that."

"I think that the foreman, Grant Sanders, can be trusted to keep things running until decisions are made as to the future of Bonner Ranch."

"It must be sold."

"Perhaps, but Josh loves ranching. He'd be far happier here than in town."

"Custis, are you crazy? I'm not about to let that eleven-year-old live here alone."

"I was hoping you'd say that. How soon can you move out here with Josh and start looking out for him and the financial end of things?"

Nellie went over to the couch and sat down. "Do you realize that I'm fifty-three years old? I'm just an old woman far too set in my ways to start over."

"Just hold things together here for a while. There must be other relatives that can come and help."

"Not that I know of . . . oh, wait," Nellie said. "There

are a couple of Clyde's brothers in Texas. But he'd had a falling-out with them years ago. Clyde couldn't stand either one and said they were shiftless and couldn't be trusted."

"Then leave them out of the picture," Longarm decided. "Rely on Grant Sanders when it comes to the cattle and outside operations. He knows this operation inside and out. Can you keep books and records?"

"Actually, I'm quite good at that sort of thing."

"I'm glad to hear that." Longarm headed for the front door.

"Wait for me."

Before they departed, Longarm had a long discussion with the ranch foreman, explaining that Nellie would be moving in with Josh and that the payroll would be met as soon as a few financial problems were taken care of in town.

"None of us wants to leave, and there is a lot of work to do every day," Sanders told him. "So, if you can promise we ain't gonna be working for free, we'll stick just as if Mr. Bonner were alive and still giving the orders."

"I was hoping you'd say that," Longarm told the foreman. "And keep Josh busy. Work will keep bad thoughts from crowding his mind."

"We all like the kid and will look after him, Mr. Long."

"I knew you would," Longarm said, shaking the cowboy's calloused hand.

"What about you?" Sanders asked.

"I'm going after the murderers."

"I wish I could go along on that manhunt."

"I'd appreciate your help," Longarm told him, "but you're needed here. It took a lifetime for Clyde to build up this ranch. I'm counting on you to make sure that his work and dreams don't go up in smoke."

"No, sir!"

Longarm collected Josh and Nellie in the buggy, and they drove back to Denver. As they passed out of the ranch yard, Grant Sanders already had the cowboys mounted and ready to ride.

"Josh, we'll be needing you as a regular hand as soon as you get back," Sanders called out.

For the first time since Elizabeth's death, Josh smiled.

Chapter 9

When Longarm returned to Nellie's house, he wanted to leave immediately, but the woman put her foot down, saying, "Oh, no, you don't! You are dirty, unshaven, and unkempt. I used to shave and barber my father, and that's what I'm going to do to you . . . after you've had a bath."

"But Nellie, I've got to get out there and start investigating," Longarm protested.

"What is a few hours going to matter? The men you seek committed their heinous crime almost two weeks ago. Now go in there and take a bath, then come out and I'll cut your hair and shave your beard."

"You can cut the hair," he allowed, "but I'm keeping the beard."

"Why!"

"Because I'm going to be hunting men that might recognize me. If they knew about the Bonner Ranch payroll schedule, you can bet that at least one of them would know who I am. With a beard, I'll be harder to fix. Even a moment's hesitation trying to decide if I am Custis Long might make the difference between living or dying."

"He's right," Josh said. "Custis is well known in Denver. Maybe with a beard people won't recognize him so easily."

"Josh," Longarm said, reaching into his pants and getting the key to his room. "Run over to my place and bring back some clean clothes. Underwear, pants, shirt . . . the works. It doesn't make any sense to take a bath, then climb back into the same filthy clothes that I've been wearing so long."

"Sure."

Longarm's rooming house was only two blocks away, and the boy had been there many times. As Josh was leaving, Longarm yelled, "Bring back a new suit coat, hat, and vest too."

"Will do!" Josh called out as he headed outside.

"I'm not sure that he's ready to be running loose yet," Nellie fussed.

"He'll be fine," Longarm assured her. "You can't over-protect the boy or he'll wind up fearful. You have to give him plenty of rein."

"I'll see that he has all the freedom he needs out on the ranch," Nellie promised. "But here in town . . . well, I worry. What if one of those killers happened to have seen him watching them from the upstairs window as they were filling their saddlebags and gunnysacks?"

"Then they'd have come back into the house, climbed the stairs, and shot Josh to death," Longarm told her. "There is no doubt about that whatsoever."

Nellie wasn't pleased, but she must have seen the logic of Custis's reasoning because she snapped, "Go ahead and bathe, then we'll trim your mane while we wait for Josh to return. I swear, you remind me of a stray mongrel."

"I feel like one that has been kicked a few times," Longarm told her as he went into the bathroom.

He undressed while the tub was filling with hot water, and examined his battered body in Nellie's bathroom mirror. What he saw was a man who had lost a good deal of weight and who looked as if he'd been to war. His shoulder was still purple from the mule's kick, and his thigh wound was scabbed over but very sore.

I should rest a few days and eat everything I can stomach in order to get my weight and strength back before I head off on this manhunt. But I couldn't stand to sit around. Four men are out there somewhere. Maybe they've already spent the Bonner Ranch payroll and are feeling the need to rob and kill another wealthy family. But maybe they're living high on the hog right here in Denver, just thumbing their noses at the law and thinking that they got away with it all. And I wonder how much money was in that safe in addition to the monthly ranch payroll. Maybe thousands of dollars. And the personal items they took ... well, even if they were hocked in a pawnshop or sold as stolen goods, they'd still bring a few thousand dollars. Why, that diamond-horseshoe ring of Clyde's had to be worth a small fortune itself, not to mention the engagement ring that they stole from Elizabeth after killing her.

When Longarm thought about Elizabeth Bonner, his throat tightened and he felt a sick emptiness. He'd lost the woman of his dreams.

You can't get her back ... but you can get even. So focus on revenge, because there are few more powerful emotions than hatred and revenge.

After his bath, Nellie cut his dark locks and trimmed his beard, clipping off the wet hair with a pair of barber's scissors. "I used to be very good at this," she said as she worked. "I'd give Clyde a haircut every time I went out to the ranch. I kept it up long after he could afford to have his hair cut by a real barber because he thought I did a better job."

"I don't much care how good or bad a job you do," Longarm said glumly. "I just want to get dressed and hit the street."

"And you really think that you will be lucky enough to

71

find some of the items stolen from the ranch house?"

"Probably not," he confessed. "What I am sure of is that I'll not leave Denver until I'm sure that the killers have moved elsewhere. When it comes to this town, I know who is shady and deals in stolen goods. Nellie, if the things stolen from the ranch are in this town, I'll find at least one of them."

"If you do, I think you ought to bring Mr. Vail and the federal authorities in on the case."

"Not a chance. They'd flush the killers and we'd never find them."

"But what if you found something that could lead to their arrest but were . . ."

"Killed?"

"Yes," the woman said quietly. "You may think that having a beard will disguise you from the killers, but I'm not so sure. You're such a big man that you attract notice. It wouldn't take long for the word to get out in this town that Custis Long has turned in his badge and is out to gun down the Bonner Ranch killers."

"You may be right," he conceded. "But if that's the case, they might decide to try and ambush me. If they do and fail, I've got them."

"Or they've got you!" Nellie began to trim his beard. "Either you are the stupidest man I've ever known, or the toughest and bravest. Custis, the people that killed dear Elizabeth and Clyde are ruthless killers. They are not a bunch of drunken fools who did something on the spur of the moment. I wouldn't talk like this in front of Josh, but these people are professionals."

"I know."

"Then you ought to know better than to talk about setting yourself up for an ambush in the hope that it fails."

"There is no time to be cautious," he replied. "The trail is already cold and it's growing more so every day. I have to take chances."

"I understand that, but it makes no sense to get yourself

72

killed. Why, just look at you now. You've a broken shoulder and a bum leg."

"Both of which are getting better every day."

"Humph!" Nellie snorted as her scissors worked even faster. "If you won't use good sense in protecting yourself, try to imagine what your death would do to Josh. Why, he'd likely go completely to pieces if you were ambushed and killed by the very same bunch that took away his mother and grandfather!"

"Nellie, if anything happens to me, go to Billy Vail and put both yourself and Josh under his protection."

"I can understand why Josh would be in danger, but why me?"

"Because the killers would assume that Josh gave you some pretty detailed descriptions. And it's clear that those people are not the kind to leave any loose ends dangling like a hangman's rope."

"Just stay alive and healthy."

"I will."

When Josh returned with his clothes, Longarm dressed and studied himself in the mirror. His face was gaunt and his cheeks were sunken, but his full black beard covered most of that. It was the dark circles under both his eyes that reminded him how hard the past few weeks had been. Despite that, Longarm felt himself capable of going after Elizabeth's killers. But he needed to get rid of his sling because that would be a dead giveaway.

Instead of that damned sling, I'll support my shoulder by hooking my thumb into my gun belt, he decided, doing exactly that.

The shoulder felt stiff and it ached, but the really sharp pain was gone. As for his leg wound, well, he'd try not to limp anymore. Without a limp or his sling and wearing these clean clothes and a full beard, Longarm figured he might pass as a stranger unless someone knew him quite well.

"Will you be coming back tonight for supper?" Nellie

asked, worry written all over her round and pleasant face.

"I don't think so. I'll eat out."

"But you will keep in close touch," she said, her tone of voice leaving no doubt this was expected.

"Yes." Longarm turned to Josh. "You're gonna be going out to the ranch in a few days. But I'll get word to you just as soon as I make some progress."

"You promise?"

"I give you my word on it," Longarm replied.

It was midafternoon and Longarm's leg was really throbbing with pain as he made his way from one Denver pawnshop to the next. He had jotted down a list of seven such businesses, knowing that there were a few of which he might not be aware. So far, he'd visited five of the largest and most disreputable, figuring he'd start where the odds were the highest of seeing any familiar goods stolen from the Bonner ranch house.

The sixth pawnshop was like the first five, only smaller and more disorganized. Longarm saw the usual array of pawned goods ranging from guns and rifles to saddles and even bear traps.

"Afternoon," the proprietor said in greeting. "What can I sell you today?"

"I'm just looking," Longarm replied, eyes missing nothing.

"For anything in particular?"

"Well," he said, "I am partial to rings. Do you have any?"

"Does a beaver eat wood?" The man moved along behind his counter. "By the way, my name is Eli. Come over here and I'll show you what we have to offer."

The rings Longarm was shown were mostly simple gold and silver bands, although a few included semiprecious stones. "See anything you like?"

"Nope. I'm looking for something . . . special."

Eli was a short, sweaty man with a prominent gold tooth

74

and a waxed mustache. "Special as in expensive?"

"Mister, I want a ring that will turn heads and make everyone think I'm rich."

"I might have a ring like that coming in today or tomorrow."

"What do you mean, 'might'?"

Eli leaned over his glass counter, and Longarm smelled whiskey on his breath. "Well," the man said in a confidential tone, "there was a gent in here yesterday that said he had some high-class jewelry and needed quick cash."

Longarm pretended not to be particularly interested. "What kind of jewelry?"

"A pair of diamond rings. He described one as being an engagement ring . . . which I gather has no interest for you."

"I expect to remain a bachelor."

"Wise man."

"And the other?"

"Very special, from what the man said. He said he wouldn't take a cent less than three hundred dollars for that one."

"A lot of money."

"Damn right! Why, all the rings you see before you ain't worth that much put together, so of course I told him I wasn't interested. But the fella insisted this particular ring was worth at least a thousand dollars. He said he'd bring it in today or tomorrow right about closing time and I'd pay his price when I laid my eyes upon it."

"So what did you say?"

Eli threw up his hands. "What do I have to lose by looking? The man sounded so confident that maybe the ring is worth a fortune. I won't know until I put it under a jeweler's ring. I know a real rock when I see one."

"Did he describe this ring?"

"No. Just said that it was gold with diamonds and worth a lot of money. I told him that I rarely sold a ring worth more than a few hundred dollars. No offense, mister, but most of my customers are not what you would call prosperous. Now, what I want to know is if this is in *your* price range."

"I could go to three hundred."

"You have to pay me at least a few bucks more than I paid for it, or else why would I waste my time?"

"Look," Longarm said, "if that man returns, tell him that you have someone in mind and would he leave it on consignment."

"I won't do that."

"Why not?"

"I pay cash and I expect cash in return. I'm not interested in that consignment crap. It's nothing but a big headache. I've seen people in my line of work go out of business because they lost or spent the consignment money. Uh-uh. I do nothing but cash."

"Makes sense," Longarm said. "But the ring interests me. If it is a good deal, buy it and I'll probably want it enough to insure you make a reasonable profit."

"I'll keep you in mind," Eli promised, eyeing him up and down. "Are you sure you don't need anything else?"

Longarm spied a handsome pocketknife. "How much do you want for that knife?"

"The one with the white bone handle?"

"That's right."

Eli removed it from his case. "It's a beauty, isn't it! The steel is excellent. You can tell that by the sharpness of its blade."

"How much?"

"Not much. Mister, you could shave with that blade."

Longarm ran the blade along the back of his hand, and sure enough, shaved himself clean. "How much?"

"I could let go of it for . . . oh, ten dollars."

"For that kind of money I can buy a new Barlow."

"This one is far better than a Barlow. Listen, since you're interested in the ring and I want you to be happy, I'll let you have this knife for only nine dollars."

"Eight dollars even and it's a sale."

Eli's expression grew pained. Finally, he shrugged and said, "Oh, what the hell? All right."

Longarm extracted a ten-dollar bill from his wallet and handed it to the man, who reached into his pocket and brought out his money clip to make change. "Nice clip," Longarm said, recognizing it as belonging to Clyde Bonner.

"Solid silver," Eli told him, handing Longarm two dollars.

"Have you owned it long?"

"As a matter of fact, I got it from the same man that has that big diamond ring we were discussing. I expect he must be fencing stolen goods, but what the hell do I care? I don't steal anything and I don't ask questions as to ownership. If I did, I'd soon be out of business."

"I understand," Longarm replied, watching Clyde Bonner's expensive money clip disappear. "Maybe I'll hang around and see if that fella with the ring comes back."

"Suit yourself, but he might never return. You know how some men like to make talk like they have money and are important."

"True. But he did have that solid silver money clip."

"And an engagement ring. I bought that along with the money clip."

Longarm cleared his throat. "Mind if I see it?"

"But you just swore you'd stay a bachelor."

"Mister, a fella never knows when he might just stumble into the right girl and change his mind."

Eli snorted with derision. "Keep your money and stay single! Let me tell you something. I been married *four* times, and every one of my former wives cost me a bundle. Why, I used to own a bunch of pawnshops both here and in Kansas City! My ex-wives got the other ones, but they don't know shit about the business, so I'll eventually buy them out at fifty cents on the dollar. But I can't tell you how that galls my fat ass."

"I'll bet it does."

"You still want to see the engagement ring? The diamonds are real but they're small. Actually, the ring isn't all that special. Probably cost the poor sucker less than a hundred dollars from a downtown jeweler, and I could let it go for . . . oh, seventy dollars cash."

It cost me one hundred and fifty, you horse's ass.

"Here," Eli said. "Some fella didn't exactly break the bank on this one, but at least he didn't buy glass like a lot of men do and then try to pass it off as the real thing."

It was Elizabeth's ring. Longarm couldn't stop his fingers from trembling as Eli pressed it into his hands.

"You nervous or something?"

"No."

"Then why are your fingers shakin'?"

"I get shaky when I miss a meal."

"Big, broad-shouldered guy like you?"

"That's right."

"Huh. Well, what do you think of that one?"

"I'll buy it," Longarm said without hesitation.

Eli chuckled. "Ah-ha! You must have some little lady you want to get into bed and you think this cheap little ring will do the trick! Ain't that right?"

Longarm managed to nod as he paid the man and placed the ring in his vest pocket.

Eli glanced at the clock on the wall. "I close in forty-five minutes. Maybe you ought to go get something to eat since you're shaking so bad."

"Good idea. I'll be back right before closing."

"Bring a bundle of cash in case that man shows up with a ring that will turn heads," Eli shouted as Longarm hurried outside.

He walked half a block down the street, then stopped and reached into his vest pocket, bringing out Elizabeth's ring. It was all that Longarm could do to hold back his bitter tears as he rubbed the engagement ring back and forth between his thumb and forefinger.

I could have asked Billy Vail to send a man over and confiscate this along with the money clip, but what if someone had purchased it before that happened? I'd have lost a part of what Elizabeth and I were together.

Longarm took a deep breath and returned the ring to his vest. He went into a tobacco shop and bought a box of cigars, good ones rather than his usual cheap cheroots. Then he stepped back outside and lit one of them to smoke. From where he stood, he had a clear view of Eli's pawnshop. He regretted not asking for a description of the man he sought, but that might have been too obvious and he'd have aroused suspicions.

I'll wait right until Eli closes. And I'll be here when he reopens in the morning, if necessary. I can almost smell my man. He's close. Maybe he's the Scot. Either way, he's a dead man.

Chapter 10

Longarm waited in vain that afternoon. He waited until he saw Eli closing shop, then headed back to Aunt Nellie's place for a good meal and night's sleep. The minute he arrived at the older woman's house, she and Josh wanted to know all about his visits to the pawnshops. After telling them about his good luck, Longarm removed the engagement ring from his vest.

"It's true that I didn't pay a lot of money for this ring. But I was going to buy her a big wedding ring, one a lot more expensive."

"Custis," Nellie said in her gentlest voice. "You know that Liz didn't care all that much about wealth and appearances. It was you she wanted, not some big, gaudy ring."

"I know."

"Mom really loved you," Josh said, with his own eyes brimming with tears. "You could have given her a ring made of tin and she'd have worn it proudly."

Longarm had to leave the room for a while. Later, he ate a huge meal and went to bed early, saying, "Josh, let's just pray that the man with your grandfather's ring returns to hock it tomorrow. If he does, I need to take him alive so I can find out where the others are hiding. You understand that, don't you?"

"I guess. But you promised . . ."

"I know what I promised," Longarm said. "But I also promised I'd hunt them down to the last man. This fella that I'm hoping to capture tomorrow is the key to getting all the others, so I can't kill him."

"Then you'll turn him in and the feds will take over the chase instead of you." Josh frowned. "Don't you see that?"

"Yeah," Longarm said, "I do. Tell you what. I'll think on it tonight and maybe we can come up with something."

Nellie stamped her foot down hard. "Now listen to me and listen good! I don't exactly know what is going on between you, and maybe I don't want to know. All I'm sure of is that you can't execute someone no matter who you are or what the reason. Custis, you turned in your badge but not your humanity."

"Yes, ma'am."

"So tomorrow if that fella does show up, you have a legal and moral obligation to try and arrest . . . not kill . . . the man. If you kill him, you will be no better than he is."

Longarm's hands knotted at his sides. "With all due respect, he *murdered* Josh's mother and grandmother and my intended wife. Revenge is in order."

"Oh?" Nellie asked, eyebrows raising in question. "And what happens when you are tried for murder and sent to prison? Is *that* what you want?"

"Of course not!"

"Then you had better do some real hard thinking tonight and come to understand the consequences you'd face if you are considering killing the man."

"Custis, you gave me your word," Josh said. "And if you won't live up to it, then let me have a gun and after he tells you where the others are, I'll kill him myself."

Longarm was caught in a trap. Nellie was right. If he executed a killer in front of witnesses, he'd likely be sent to prison and maybe even the gallows. But at the same time, dammit, killing a cold-blooded murderer was not the same as killing innocent people.

I'll just have to let it play out tomorrow and see what happens. Could be my man might not even return to the pawnshop and then I'll have to start from scratch again. I sure hope he comes so that we can let the chips fall where they may.

He awoke at seven o'clock feeling surprisingly refreshed and very hungry. Longarm dressed and went into the bathroom to study his face. The dark circles around his eyes were fading, and he rather liked himself with the trimmed beard and mustache. He rotated his shoulder, and that was feeling much better, as was his bad leg.

And it's just about time.

Longarm hadn't fretted about the dilemma he might face this day, and he felt sure that if one of the killers showed up to pawn that diamond-studded horseshoe ring, events would unfold to his liking.

"Mornin'," he said to Nellie when he entered her kitchen. "Whatever you're cooking smells mighty tasty."

"It's just pancakes and bacon with fried mush and toast. Coffee is on the stove, so help yourself."

Longarm did just that. The coffee was strong enough to corrode a horseshoe, but that was exactly how he liked it.

"Sit down," Nellie ordered, bringing over a stack of hot food. "Now, you eat all of that and don't give me any lip."

"You're kinda testy this mornin', ain't ya?"

"I have a right to be after what I saw pass between you and Josh last night."

"Now Nellie, it's going to be all right."

"Sure it is! You're going to arrest that man and haul him down to the Federal Building for questioning. And then maybe you'll ask for your badge back because, to my way of thinking, that's the only thing you can do well."

"You mean being a United States deputy marshal?"

"That's right. I know that Elizabeth didn't like it, but

she's gone now and I think the best thing for you is to pin on the badge and go after those killers. That way, if you have to plug a couple of the bastards through the gizzard, at least you'll have killed 'em in the line of duty."

"That's how you figure it, huh?" Longarm said around a mouthful of pancake.

"That's right."

"Well, maybe I'll just do that. Billy would love me to come back."

"So make us both happy and do it."

"I'll put some thought to it," Longarm promised.

He ate everything on his plate and asked for seconds. When he finished his third cup of coffee, Longarm made use of his napkin and said, "Thanks, Nellie. It's gettin' on toward nine o'clock, which should be the time that Eli opens his pawnshop. I'd like to be there a few minutes early in case our man is in a hurry.

"I'll tell Josh good-bye."

"Better let him sleep," Nellie said. "He needs his rest."

"Okay. But I'll peek in on him in case he's awake."

Longarm found his coat and hat, then checked his gun before he went to check on the boy. But when he looked inside Josh's bedroom, it was empty. The window curtains were fluttering, and Longarm hurried over to the window and looked outside.

"Nellie!"

She hurried in to join him. "He's gone!"

"That's right." Longarm scowled. "Maybe he just got restless and went for a walk."

"Then why would he sneak out the window?"

"I can't answer that one."

"You don't think that Josh went out to ... oh, my Gawd! Custis, maybe he intends to try and kill that man!"

"How? I'll be there to stop him."

"But what if he is hiding and ambushes the man before you can identify him?" Nellie asked, panic building in her voice. "He could do it, you know."

"Does he have a gun?"

Nellie spun around and hurried into the kitchen. She bent under the sink and felt around for a moment, then said, "I had a gun hidden in there. It's missing."

"You hid it in your kitchen?"

"Sure. That's where I spend most of my time. Josh must have found and taken it last night. Custis, you hurry over to that pawnshop and find that boy! Don't you dare let him shoot anyone!"

"I won't," Longarm vowed as he strode for the front door.

It was four blocks to Eli's pawnshop and despite the twinge in his thigh, compliments of the knife wound, Longarm covered them in near record-time. He was relieved to see that the shop wasn't open yet.

Longarm scanned the already busy streets, searching for Josh but not seeing him anywhere among the dozens of pedestrians. He frowned, and decided he had best move on down the street a few doors so that he didn't look too anxious or conspicuous. The man with the ring would be on his guard and might sense a trap.

The minutes dragged by slowly until Longarm finally saw Eli plod up to the door of his business, then unlock the door and disappear inside.

Where is Josh? Relax. Maybe he really did go for a harmless walk, leaving by the window to avoid a chance meeting with a reporter.

During the first hour that Eli was open, Longarm watched three men enter his shop and exit counting cash. Two of them hocked rifles and one a guitar. Longarm knew that none of these men was the killer he so desperately sought.

And then, he got lucky. Just a few minutes before noon, a short, powerful young man wearing a black derby hurried past him and swept inside the pawnshop.

That's got to be the one. Got to be!

Longarm had started to move toward the pawnshop when, suddenly, Josh bolted out from between a pair of buildings and sprinted into Eli's business, slamming the door in his wake.

"No!" Longarm cried, rushing forward even as he heard a cry of pain and then a gunshot.

He burst inside to see Eli clutching his arm, blood pouring out from under his sleeve. Even worse, the killer had a gun pressed to Josh's skull while choking the kid with his powerful left forearm.

Longarm took aim on the man and they froze in a Mexican standoff where there would be no winners, only dead losers.

"Drop it!" the killer shouted, cocking the hammer of his gun and grinding it into Josh's skull. "Drop it or this boy dies! All I want here is money. No one has to die unless you get stupid!"

Longarm had no choice but to drop his six-gun.

"Down on the floor! Both of you!"

Eli was ready to faint. His face was ashen and he wobbled as he joined Longarm on the floor.

"If either of you so much as quiver, this boy gets it in the head."

"Don't shoot him," Longarm pleaded, hearing the sound of Eli's cash register being opened.

"Hey, you got a safe in the back room filled with money?"

"No," Eli grated. "That's all there is. I swear it!"

The man laughed harshly. "I never meant to sell you that ring for a lousy three hundred dollars. It was just bait to get you to carry more cash today!"

Longarm pressed his hand under his chest, wiggling his fingers toward his hideout derringer. His broken shoulder had begun to throb painfully, but he didn't care so long as he could rearm himself. This man wasn't going to allow them to live and possibly identify him to the law. He and his gang hadn't allowed the Bonner family to live, and there was no reason to expect him to have had a change of heart.

Longarm heard glass shatter, and knew that the killer was breaking open the jewelry cases and filling his pockets.

He's working fast. I've got maybe one or two minutes before he's ready to leave us with bullets in our heads.

His fingers found his derringer, and as the man came around from behind the counter still stuffing his pockets and holding Josh as a shield, Longarm yanked the two-shot derringer out from under his body.

"You—"

They both fired at exactly the same moment, but Josh was squirming and fighting for his life, and he must have knocked the killer's aim off slightly, because only one bullet found its mark. Longarm emptied the second round from the derringer, and the killer and thief crashed over backward, still struggling to raise his gun.

"Gawdamn you!" Josh screamed, pulling Nellie's derringer from his pocket and emptying it almost point-blank into the man's face.

When the authorities arrived, they were told it was just a holdup gone bad. Eli would survive, and Longarm and Josh, after answering questions, were allowed to go home.

"I'm sorry," the boy said. "We needed to take him alive so he could tell us where the others are hiding, didn't we?"

"Yes, but that's all right."

"What do you mean?"

Longarm reached into his coat and removed a bloody wallet. "I got this off his body. No identification. I also emptied all his pockets."

"And?"

"Along with the usual things you'd expect to find on a man, he was carrying a room key."

"To which hotel?"

"I don't know, but it is kind of elaborate." Longarm

placed the wallet back in his pocket and produced the room key. "I'd guess there are less than a half-dozen hotels in Denver fancy enough to give this kind of key to their customers."

"Can I go looking with you?" Josh asked.

Longarm took a deep breath. "I guess so. It's probably safer to have you with me than to wonder where you'll suddenly pop up and maybe gum up the works."

"Yeah," Josh said. "I'm still shaking. I never killed a man before."

"And you didn't today," Longarm told him. "I killed that man. He was dead when your shots hit him."

"Are you sure?"

"Yes."

The boy expelled a deep breath. "You know, I'm kinda glad you killed him instead of me. I hated him and he was probably gonna do us all in, but I . . ."

"Yeah," Longarm said, putting his arm across Josh's shoulder. "I know."

87

Chapter 11

By the time that they reached the Saxony Hotel, Longarm and Josh had worked out a little plan they'd use when they approached each registration desk. Longarm would take a seat in the lobby while Josh, looking innocent and excited, would rush up to the desk and announce that he'd "found" a room key. He'd then ask if it belonged to one of the hotel's guests, as if he were hoping to reap a finder's reward.

"If the clerk recognizes the key," Longarm said, "you signal to me and I'll come by and act as if I overheard the conversation. Then I'll pat my pockets and announce that it is *my* key! I'll act so grateful I'll even offer you a reward."

"You will?"

"Sure. Then I'll turn and head upstairs with a smile on my face. Once up in the hallways, I'll just use the key until it turns a room lock."

"What do I do?"

"You go to Aunt Nellie's and wait," Longarm said, not wanting the boy anywhere nearby when he finally located the right hotel.

"All right," Josh said. "But I don't see why we couldn't

just show the desk clerk the key and ask him if it belongs to the hotel."

"Because, if it did, he'd expect you to just hand it over."

"Yeah, I guess he would at that."

"Listen," Longarm said. "Your role is very important. Just do like we've agreed and it will all work out just fine."

"Whatever you say. Are you going to ask for your badge back like Aunt Nellie wants?"

"I don't know."

"If you kill 'em slow," Josh said, looking worried, "would that mean *you'd* become an outlaw?"

Longarm frowned and laid his hand on the kid's shoulder. "Josh, when I said I'd kill them slow, I was pretty upset. I'm going to kill them, all right, but I can't bring myself to make them suffer."

"Will you still piss on their miserable dead bodies?"

Longarm had to smile. "I expect not."

"Well," Josh reasoned, "just as long as you kill them all."

"I already got the one at the pawnshop."

"What if they . . . they somehow kill you?"

"Won't happen."

"But what if they did?" Josh insisted. "Could I go after them myself?"

Longarm wasn't one to think about what-ifs, but he could see that Josh was very serious and so he took his time in forming his reply. "Look. If I were to get killed, then I'd want you to look up Marshal Billy Vail and tell him everything you know about your mom's killers. He'd take the case over himself and not rest until they were either dead or headed for the gallows."

"Okay."

"Now," Longarm said, "I'm going to buy a newspaper and wander into that hotel and sit down in one of those big, plush lobby chairs. As soon as I've done that, you rush in acting all excited and show our key to the desk clerk."

"All right."

Things went as expected. The hotel registration clerk was courteous to Josh and after a glance at the key, politely explained that it did not belong to one of their guests. "But it's obviously a hotel key," he offered, "I'd suggest that you try the El Condor Hotel located just up the street."

"Thanks," Josh said, hurrying back outside.

But their key did not belong to the El Condor either. Nor did it belong to the next three hotels they visited. However, when Josh went up to the desk clerk at the Embassy Manor, their luck changed.

"Yes, that's one of our room keys. Where did you find it?" the clerk asked.

"Outside on the street."

"Give it to me and I'll see that it is returned to the gentleman whose room it belongs to," the uniformed clerk said, reaching out for the key.

From his seat in the lobby, Longarm saw the boy take a quick step back and heard him say, "Sir, I'd like to return it to him myself."

"That's quite impossible. Give me the key."

Josh backed farther away from the registration desk, and the clerk hurried out after him. Longarm was barely able to intercede. "Excuse me! Did I overhear the boy say that he found one of your room keys?"

The clerk was brought up short, and didn't seem to appreciate Longarm's intrusion. He frowned and stammered, "Why, yes. But what—"

"I just lost my key to my room upstairs and was outside looking around. And now, this fine lad has found it. Thank you!"

Josh gave him a big grin. "You're welcome, sir."

"Here," Longarm said, handing Josh a dollar. "You are obviously a fine, enterprising lad and I believe in rewarding honesty."

"Thank you!" Josh exclaimed, shoving the dollar into his pocket and hurrying outside.

"Nice lad," Longarm said, turning to the agitated hotel clerk, then starting to head for the stairs.

The man followed him to the base of the stairs. "Excuse me."

Longarm turned. "Yes?"

"Sir, I don't recall you being . . ."

"Ooooops!" Longarm cried, dragging out his pocket watch. "I'm late and must hurry upstairs to get ready for a dinner engagement."

"But . . ."

Longarm didn't wait around for the interrogation he sensed was in store. He bounded up the long, spiral staircase. When he reached the second landing, he looked back down into the lobby and saw that the clerk was still watching him. Longarm gave the man his most winning smile, then marched down the hall as if he had been staying on this floor for several days, if not weeks.

At the end of the hall, he turned and looked back, half expecting to see the curious clerk. But the man had returned to the registration desk, so Longarm began to slip his key into one door lock after the next as he worked his way swiftly down the hall.

"Excuse me! Did you forget your room number?"

Longarm looked up to see a heavyset man in his fifties standing in his open doorway with a newspaper in his hands. The gentleman wore a frown and was studying Longarm closely.

"I . . . ah . . . was just leaving actually."

"Oh?" the man said, cocking his head a little to one side. "I am sure that I saw you try several doors."

"No, you are quite mistaken."

"I think not."

Longarm sighed. "I think so."

"I find your behavior very suspicious." The portly man handed his newspaper to someone behind him, then said, "Sir, I'm afraid that you need to accompany me downstairs so that we can make certain that you belong in this hotel."

91

"How dare you!" Longarm snapped, striding up to the man. "Of course I belong here."

"Then this business will only take a moment."

Longarm became indignant and attempted to bluff the man into going back into his room. "I find your insinuation to be insulting and outrageous!"

"Outrageous or not, I don't think you belong here," the man said, not backing down at all, and in fact becoming even more insistent. "My name is Hiram Barnaby, and I have been robbed once before. So, we are going downstairs this very minute."

Longarm could see that Barnaby was not going to let him alone. No, he was going to make a scene and cause a big commotion. That simply would not do in this case, so Longarm did the only thing he could think of to do. He threw a punch with every intention of knocking the man unconscious. His fist came up in a short, powerful arc, and it struck Hiram Barnaby at the point of his chin and sent him backward into his room. Longarm jumped forward and delivered a crunching overhand right to the side of the man's head, knocking him out cold.

"Nosy old bastard," Longarm muttered, rubbing his knuckles.

"Don't move or I'll shoot you dead!"

Longarm froze, not even daring to roll his eyes sideways toward the voice. He needn't have bothered because a beautiful young woman, naked to the waist, stepped into his view clutching a small but ominous-looking revolver.

"Who are you?" she asked, studying him closely. "A thief?"

"No."

"Then what?"

Longarm studied her breasts, which were large and firm. Elizabeth had had breasts almost as nice.

"Mister, if you can tear your eyes off my breasts, it might just save your life. Who are you?"

"I'm . . . I'm a United States deputy marshal."

"Bullshit! I think you're a burglar."

"No, I'm a lawman. Well, I was up until a couple of days ago."

The woman sat down and crossed her legs, gun still trained on Longarm. "You got a cigarette while I listen to your bullshit story?"

"I don't smoke cigarettes, but I do have a couple of cigars."

"I like cigars even better than cigarettes."

"Who are you?" he asked.

"Call me . . . Trixie. Light a cigar for me and don't try anything funny. I want to hear your story before I march you downstairs so they can have you taken to jail."

Longarm lit a cheroot and handed it to the young woman. Trixie had long, flaxen hair, and her features were strikingly similar to Elizabeth. *But this one is a prostitute while Elizabeth was a lady. Big, big difference.*

"Mind if I light one for myself?" he asked.

"Go ahead. Then start talking and if you lie to me again, I might shoot you myself and claim you broke in here after knocking out Mr. Barnaby and tried to force yourself on me. The law would believe a story like that."

"I expect they might also ask what you are doing here."

"What does that mean?"

He shrugged. "Only that you don't look like that man's wife."

She snorted. "Thank Gawd for that, at least. Hiram H. Barnaby is as rich as a king, but I can't stand him."

"But you'll take his money in exchange for giving him a little pleasure. Right?"

"I'm a working girl," Trixie said. "And believe me, I have earned my money these last couple of days."

Longarm glanced down at the man he'd knocked silly. "He doesn't look like he has that much in him."

"He don't," she said with obvious disgust, "but I had to work real hard to help him get a stiff one. Then he wanted to play silly make-believe games. Would you believe he had us both making baby talk while we were trying to do it!"

"I'm sure it was pure hell," Longarm said cryptically.

"I'm the best in town because I'm not afraid to earn my money," Trixie said with pride as she exhaled a smoke ring. "Start talking and don't feed me any lies. I know how to use this gun."

"I'm sure that you do," he told her, deciding at the same time to tell her the truth because the beautiful woman was obviously too clever to be fooled. "My name is Custis Long. I was supposed to have been married this month to Miss Elizabeth Bonner. She and her father, along with their household staff, were recently murdered out at their big cattle ranch."

"Say, even I heard about that. And you're the rich woman's fiancé?"

"I was," Longarm said, his voice dropping. "Now, I'm just trying to find out who killed her so that I can kill them."

"You got any proof about what you're saying?"

"I gave up my badge, but I might have some identification in my wallet."

"Then let's see it."

Longarm started to reach for his hideout derringer, but changed his mind. He didn't want to harm or perhaps even kill this woman, and he'd always been taught never to point a gun at someone unless you were prepared to do both. So he did extract his wallet, and damned if he didn't find one of Elizabeth's old love letters. She'd written him several, but this one had been so moving that he'd carried it close to his heart.

"What's that?"

"A letter from Elizabeth."

Trixie looked curious. "Read it."

"I'd rather not."

"Well, you'd better!"

"It's very personal."

"So is this gun in my hand."

"Okay," Longarm agreed. "I'll read . . . the first couple lines."

Dear Custis: Do you have any idea how much I love you? Does a flower have any idea how much it needs the gentle rain and the sunshine that glistens upon its petals? I love you so much that I am afraid sometimes that my heart would break if ever I should—

Longarm's voice cracked and died. The overpowering sense of his personal loss was so intense he couldn't read another word. "Trixie, shoot me if you have to because I can't read anymore."

"Let me see the letter."

He gave it to her and as Trixie read, Longarm saw that her eyes began to glisten. She got so choked up that she couldn't finish it either. Sniffling and blinking back tears, the woman choked out, "Jeezus, that is romantic. Custis, you were telling the truth. Only a woman could write something that good. I'd give anything if I could write romantic shit like that."

"Me too," Longarm said, retrieving his letter.

Trixie expelled a shuddering sigh. "You and that rich gal must have really been in love."

"We were."

The woman waved her gun at the unconscious man. "And you think old spaghetti-dick there was one of the men who murdered Miss Bonner and her family?"

"No, I do not."

"Then why did you hit him like that?"

"Let me explain."

"Okay, but that letter cut me to the gizzard. I need a drink. Would you like one too?"

The letter had also affected him powerfully, and Longarm realized he would have been better off to burn it. "I guess a drink might help."

95

"Then you tell Trixie all about her . . . if you don't mind."

Longarm poured the whiskey, which was superb. He drank and discovered he really needed to talk. So he told the sympathetic prostitute everything about himself and Elizabeth. His anguished words poured out in a torrent. By the time that he was finished, they were practically crying on each other's shoulder.

Trixie was hugging him. "Honey, do you feel better now?"

"I do."

"I sure wish that I was Elizabeth Bonner and you were marrying me. I'm half drunk and half in love with you already."

It wasn't until he tried to stand that Longarm realized that they'd drained half the bottle and that he was tipsy. "I'd better go."

She slipped into a dress and buttoned it up the front. "Where?"

"Aunt Nellie is putting me up."

"I got a place two doors down the hallway."

He looked sideways at Trixie. "You live here?"

"Sure. My room isn't quite as big or fancy as this one, but it's nice. You see, in exchange for the exclusive privilege of entertaining the hotel's guests, half of what I make goes to the hotel. I also get a free room with fresh linen supplied daily. The arrangement works for them and it works for me."

"I'm glad."

"Come on, honey," Trixie said, taking his hand. "I got another bottle down there and we'll drink and cry a little more. You need a woman's love real bad and you'll feel a lot better for it tomorrow."

"I'm not too sure." He pulled back from her. "I . . . I'm not even sure that I can be with a woman, and I won't pay for it, Trixie."

"It's on the house," Trixie announced as they stepped

over the man who was just beginning to stir, before locking the door behind them. "You rescued me from that pompous old fart, and now I'm going to rescue you from the past."

Longarm tried to figure that one out, but gave it up halfway down the hallway. Trixie led him into her room, then shut and locked the door.

"You've got good taste," he said, looking around at the expensive furnishings.

"Yeah, I think I do," she said, removing his coat, vest, and shirt.

"Easy on the shoulder."

"What happened to it?" she asked.

"Got kicked by a mule and broke it."

A few minutes later, she saw his thigh and her eyes widened. "Jeez, what happened to you here?"

"Knife wound."

"You have scars all over your body, Custis. It's a good thing that you changed your line of work."

"Trixie, I'm talked out," he confessed. "Could we either have another drink or see what happens when we get into bed?"

"I like the second suggestion better," she replied, removing her dress and turning back the bedcovers. "Climb in and let's see if we can take care of what ails you."

"This won't heal an aching heart."

Trixie got into bed and opened herself to him. "I know. But maybe it will make you realize that you'll want to make love again."

That was good enough for Longarm. He fell into her arms and they began kissing. Soon, his tongue was ravishing her breasts and his stiff rod was thrusting and twisting its way deep into her luscious body. Trixie wrapped her long legs around his hips and pleaded, "Come on, honey, take it fast or take it slow, but give me everything you got!"

Longarm completely gave himself up to the woman. He

97

became heady with her perfume and crazy with desire as his body drove faster and harder into her honeypot. Soon, they were gasping and Trixie was saying things to him that he'd heard before from Elizabeth. It did not matter that her groans and whisperings of love were only meant to heal the pain in his heart. All that mattered was that they were one and he was no longer alone and apart from love. He growled and went at her without thought of the past or the future, only wanting to plant his hot seed deep into her hungry body.

When the torrent of fire erupted, Longarm threw his head back and roared with pleasure and filled her, as Trixie's own body began to convulse and she wailed joyfully in the ecstasy of her own intense and powerful release.

Chapter 12

When Longarm awakened, moonlight flooded through Trixie's window. Trixie snored softly as he dressed and tiptoed out into the hallway. Then, he removed the room key from his pocket, unholstered his six-gun, and began trying out the remaining doors in the upstairs hallway.

On the fifth or six try, the key silently turned in the lock of Room 114, telling Longarm that he was about to find one or more of the men who had murdered his dear Elizabeth and her father and household staff. Longarm eased the door open, listening for the sounds of men asleep. But he heard nothing, so he crept forward until he bumped up against the foot of the bed.

They were gone.

"Damn!" he hissed, reaching into his pocket and finding a match. The match flared to reveal an unmade bed. A quick search of the abandoned room offered no clues other than cigar butts and three empty bottles of expensive scotch whiskey. Longarm rushed downstairs to the registration desk. A large pendulum clock told him that it was a quarter past four in the morning.

"When did the man in Room 114 leave?" he asked the sleepy-eyed desk clerk engrossed in a Denver newspaper.

The young man glanced up and shrugged his thin shoulders in a nonchalant attitude, saying, "Mister, I have no idea."

"Don't you have a record of some kind?"

"No."

"Let's see the registration book."

The clerk neatly folded his paper, stood up, and said, "I can't give that to you unless you are registering."

Longarm wasn't in the mood for negotiating. He hurried around the desk, grabbed the book, and opened it on the counter.

"Hey," the young hotel clerk protested, "you can't come back here!"

"Fine," Longarm replied, moving back around the counter with the book in his hands. "I'll read this out here if that makes you feel any better."

"Give that back!" the clerk exclaimed, reaching for the book.

Longarm's hand clamped on the man's wrist and he dug his thumbnail into soft flesh, driving the hotel clerk onto his toes, making him cry out.

"I think," Longarm said, "you had better start cooperating. Wouldn't you agree?"

"Yes!"

Longarm eased up on his thumb pressure. "Good. Then I'll ask you once more. When did the occupant of Room 114 leave?"

"Just after midnight. That's when my shift started."

"Describe him."

"He was ordinary-looking. Yeah, just ordinary."

Longarm's thumbnail pressed down hard. "That's not good enough."

"All right! All right! Stop hurting me!"

"Then answer my questions. What was he wearing? What did he have to say and was he alone or in company?"

"He was alone and dressed in a brown suit with a bowler on his head. I said good evening and asked if he were just going out to get some night air. He told me that he was leaving town. I thought that strange because he only carried one small satchel. But then he was headed out the door and that's the last I saw of him."

"And he said nothing more?"

The clerk shook his head. "I swear that's all the conversation we had together."

Longarm released the quivering clerk and scanned the registration book, flipping pages over one by one. "What was the man's name?"

The clerk spun around and found a card file. A moment later, he pulled a card and said, "He registered as Ed Hatch. He listed his occupation as a liquor salesman and his home town as St. Louis."

"And that's all?"

The clerk fell back in his chair. "Yes, sir. Now do you mind me asking who *you* are?"

"I'm . . . I'm just an ordinary citizen," Longarm stammered a moment before he turned and hurried back up the stairs.

This time he went over the room very carefully, looking for evidence of some kind that might give him some useful clues as to the real identity of Ed Hatch, which was probably a fictitious name. But he didn't find anything.

Longarm took a deep breath and tried to decide what to do next. Was the man who had occupied this room one of Elizabeth's killers? He might not have had a thing to do with the murder and robbery committed out at the Bonner Ranch. But somehow, Longarm suspected that he was on the right track.

"Custis?"

He turned to see a very sleepy-looking Trixie standing in her nightgown framed by the open doorway. "Yeah?"

"What are you doing?"

"Remember that key I was using to try the doors?"

"Yes."

"Well, it fit this one. Trouble is, the man who had this room has vanished."

Trixie scrubbed her eyes with the back of her hand. "I knew him."

"You did?"

"Yes." She stepped into the room, closing the door behind her. "I . . . I was in this bed more than once. The man paid me quite handsomely, but I refused to return because he was so crude and rough."

"Tell me everything you can about him."

Trixie sat down on the bed. "I need coffee."

"No time for that."

"All right. He was average-sized, but quite strong."

"Did he have an accent?"

"What?"

"An Irish or Scottish accent?"

"No."

"Was he armed?"

"Oh, sure. I saw a gun belt hanging over this bedpost, and a rifle was propped up in the corner. He was a tough one, but he paid me well."

"Did he tell you his name?"

"No." Trixie managed a half smile. "But they rarely do. Or, if they do, the name is phony. You can understand that. I mean, Trixie isn't my real name."

"Did he tell you where he was from or where he was going?"

Trixie frowned. "He was kind of secretive. But the second time I was here, he was a bit drunk and told me that he was doing some kind of a 'deal' with three other friends. He talked about one of them more than the others, and referred to him as Scotty."

"Did he say where they were staying?"

"No. But I saw two of them in the hallway more than once. I think that this was their meeting spot. A couple of times I saw them walk into the room without the boarder with them. The one I figured to be Scotty wore a red and green checkered scarf and a cap. He was big and handsome. He had dimples in his cheeks and a smile that told me he was kind of a rogue and a rascal. The other man I can't even recall."

Longarm sat down beside Trixie. "Did the one who stayed here ever mention pawnshops?"

"As a matter of fact, he did. Said he had some things he'd inherited and was turning into cash. A couple of rings and a money clip."

"He's one of them, all right," Longarm said, jumping up and starting to pace back and forth. "He was registered as Ed Hatch. But where could the man have gone in the middle of the night?"

"Maybe the gambling houses. He liked to play cards. He even showed me a deck of cards that he'd marked."

"How were they marked?"

"He'd altered the back of the cards ever so slightly." Trixie shrugged. "They were good. I wouldn't have minded having a deck of those myself. But cards aren't my game."

"This Hatch fella actually showed you these marked cards?"

"That's right. Two nights ago he rode me so hard and got so rough that I told him I wasn't going to service him anymore."

"And what did he say to that?"

"He apologized. Said he was angry because he'd lost so much money lately, but that his luck was about to change for the better. That's when he showed me the marked deck. He was sort of bragging and telling me that he was about to have a lot of money and the sight of it would make me change my mind about screwin' him again. But, Custis, it really wouldn't have. I was a little bit afraid of the son-ofabitch."

"You had every reason to be. Where did he gamble?"

"He never told me, but I saw him leave the hotel many

times and go into Palace Club just up the street. That's where I think he spent most of his time."

"Trixie, you've been a big help. Could you do me one more favor?"

"Sure. If the sonofabitch was one of the ones that killed Miss Bonner, I'd be more than glad to see him hanged or shot."

"Then get dressed and let's go over to the Palace Club. There's a good chance he isn't there at this hour, but he has to be somewhere and maybe I'll get lucky."

"What do you need me for?"

"All I'll want you to do is stick your head inside the club and, if you see him, step out and tell me where he's at. I'll take care of the rest."

"Okay," Trixie said with a yawn. "But I'm missing my beauty sleep and I'll expect a large favor in return."

"That being?"

"I don't know yet. But you can be sure part of it will be coming back to bed with me and doing exactly what I tell you to do."

"Mmmm. Sounds like fun!"

"Doesn't it, though?" she told him as she swayed down the hallway to her room.

The street outside was dimly lit by a few flickering lamps, and the only people they saw were a few drunks who had fallen asleep in the doorways. Only a few gambling halls and saloons stayed in business all night, and those that did had very few customers.

"Are you going to just walk in and gun him down?" Trixie asked.

"No. I'm going to walk in and bust his skull. Then I'll throw him over my shoulder and take him down to Cherry Creek, where I'll dump him in that cold water. After that, I'll drag him out and make him tell me where his friends are hiding."

"If he doesn't drown."

"He won't."

"Will you kill him after he talks?"

Longarm glanced down at Trixie. "You sure ask a lot of fool questions."

"Will you drown him?"

"I haven't decided yet," Longarm replied. "Now, can we stop the idle chatter?"

"I'd hardly call discussing the fate of another human being idle chatter."

"Trixie, sometimes . . . maybe a lot of times, things just unfold in their own way. You can't always plan things out. There's a good chance that Hatch or whatever his name is has left the Palace Club. But even if he is still there using his marked deck, I can't begin to predict what I'll do and then what he'll do."

"You want to kill him, though. I can tell you do."

"Yes, I do."

"If you're worried about going to jail, I'd stand up as your witness. I could say he drew his gun first or whatever you wanted me to tell the judge."

"Thanks," Longarm said. "But I'll handle things myself."

"Just don't let the sonofabitch shoot you. He probably carries a derringer and a knife."

"I'm sure he does." They stopped outside the Palace Club, and Longarm drew his gun. "Take a peek inside and tell me if you see the man."

Trixie did as she was told, and a moment later said, "He's there, all right. There are four men playing cards at a back table. Our man is the one with his back to the wall. He's wearing a brown suit."

"Thanks."

"What can I do next?"

"Go back to your room and get some sleep."

"Are you crazy! I can't do that."

"Why not?"

"Because you might get wounded and need me."

"All right. Then wait here and don't move until I come out or call for help."

"I'm armed." Trixie dragged a pistol out of her purse. "And I can hit what I aim for if it's close."

"Good."

Longarm walked into the gambling establishment, and saw that the only person in attendance other than those seated at the card table was an elderly bartender wearing red suspenders and a dirty white shirt buttoned up to his chin. The bartender saw him immediately and said, "Whiskey?"

"Why not?" Longarm replied, leaning against the bar after dropping a coin on its shiny surface.

His whiskey came, but he barely noticed as he watched the men play poker. If Hatch had been seated with his back to the front of the street, Longarm would have simply walked up and pistol-whipped the man, then taken him down to the river for questioning. But Hatch did have his back to the wall, and his eyes locked with Longarm's and held them for a moment before they dropped back down to the cards in his hand.

Longarm picked up his shot glass and strolled over to the card game. He motioned to the single empty chair, saying, "Mind if I sit in for a few hands?"

Hatch shook his head, and so did the others, to indicate they didn't care. Longarm took his seat and bought five dollars worth of chips. He noticed that Hatch was the big winner at this table, and when the man dealt him a hand, Longarm turned it over and studied the back of the cards until he recognized the faint traces of markings.

"Hey, what the hell are you doing!" Hatch snarled. "I can see your hand!"

"You could no matter how I held 'em," Longarm said.

"What the hell is that supposed to mean!"

"These cards are marked."

"The hell you say!" Hatch shouted, coming to his feet, hand streaking for his gun.

106

Longarm tossed his whiskey into Hatch's eyes, then hit him between the eyes with the empty glass. Hatch cried out in pain, and Longarm clubbed him across the forehead with his six-gun. Hatch spilled forward and when he struck the table, it overturned sending cards, money, and chips flying.

"The cards are marked," Longarm said to the other players. "Take a good, hard look and you'll see why this man was winning all your money."

It took a few moments, but when the other players finally saw the professionally marked cards, they grew incensed.

"I'm a former deputy marshal," Longarm told them. "You boys can divide up the chips and money as suits you fairly. I'm arresting this man."

"He oughta be shot or hanged!" one of the players shouted.

"Damn right he should," another yelled.

"Don't worry," Longarm assured them as he hoisted the unconscious man up and then over his good shoulder. "Justice will be served!"

Longarm stormed out of the Palace Club and Trixie fell in behind, hurrying to overtake him as he headed down toward Cherry Creek. And far off to the east, the sun was just starting to rise on another fine new day.

Chapter 13

Hatch moaned when Longarm threw him down on the bank of Cherry Creek and began slapping his face, one cheek and then the other.

"Wake up!"

The semiconscious killer's eyes fluttered open, and Longarm grabbed him by the hair and said, "Who are you and where are your friends?"

"Huh?" the man asked groggily.

Longarm was fresh out of patience, so he dragged the man into the cold water. This roused Hatch and he struggled to stand, but Longarm shoved his face under the water and then knelt on his back. The killer began to thrash violently, but Longarm's grip was as tight as a vise.

"Custis, you're drowning him!"

"Trixie, you'd better leave."

"But he can't help you if he's dead!"

Longarm ripped the man's head up from the bottom of the creek. He was choking and sputtering. "Who are you and where are your friends?" Longarm repeated.

"Go to Hell!"

Down went Hatch again, and this time Longarm sat on his back and grabbed his ears, holding his face to the mud several inches below the surface. He could feel the outlaw's chest heaving and hear his gurgling screams.

I'll give him fifteen more seconds.

"Custis, he's drowning!"

Longarm yanked the killer's head back, and there was just enough daylight to see that Hatch's face was blue and he was only semiconscious.

"Damn," Longarm swore, dragging the man out of the water and then pounding him on the back until he vomited. "Talk to me!"

The killer tried to say something, but fainted.

"Now you've gone and done it," Trixie said with exasperation. "His lungs are probably still full of water and he's dying."

"He'd better not be."

Longarm slammed his fist down a few more times on the outlaw's back, causing more creek water to erupt from his mouth. After several minutes, the killer's eyes fluttered and he gazed up at Longarm.

"If I drag you back into Cherry Creek, you're not coming out alive," Longarm vowed. "So do you want to answer my questions, or are you prepared to meet your maker?"

"I'll talk," Hatch gasped.

"First, what is your *real* name?"

"Joe. Joe Reeves."

"Where are you from?"

"El Paso."

"Who is the Scot? The one that was in charge when you murdered and robbed those people at the Bonner Ranch?"

Reeves tried to sit up, but Longarm pinned him to the mud. "I don't know what you're talking about!" Reeves shouted.

Longarm grabbed the man by the hair and started dragging him screaming and kicking back into the creek.

"Okay, his name is Ian!"

"What's his last name?"

"I swear he never told us. Ian hired us in Texas and then paid our way up here, telling us nothing."

"But you must have known he was going to use you to rob and murder."

"Rob, sure! But not murder. Me and my brother didn't know we'd be part of a family execution. I swear we didn't kill those people. Ian did!"

"Keep talking."

"Ain't nothing much else to tell you. My brother is dead. Someone shot Wade at the pawnshop."

"I killed him. And if you don't tell me what I need to know in order to find Ian and the other man that was with you at the Bonner Ranch, I'll kill you too."

"I didn't kill them poor people. Neither did my brother Wade. Sure, we were there and had guns, but it was Ian and Ned Hampton done 'em all in."

"Where are those two now?"

"I dunno." Joe Reeves sobbed and wiped his face with a muddy hand. "I figure they must have got scared and left Denver after you killed my brother. They were supposed to come by last night and we were all going away together. So I waited until after midnight and when they didn't show, I left the hotel."

"To play poker?" Longarm grabbed Reeves by the throat. "It doesn't make sense to me that someone running scared would buy into a poker game and spend the night gambling."

"I'm broke! I was hoping to turn the few dollars I had left into a good stake so that I could buy a train ticket this morning and head south."

Longarm searched the man's pockets, and all he found was a few dollars in bills and change. At least that part of Reeve's story rang true.

"Hey!" the bedraggled outlaw cried, looking past Longarm to see Trixie. "I know you!"

"Yeah, but I ain't gonna help you. Not after what you and your friends did to the Bonners."

"Please," Reeves begged. "I didn't want them people to die. Ian told us that there wasn't going to be anyone home at the ranch when we robbed the place."

"And you believed him?"

"We had no choice. Ian would have killed us if we'd tried to back out. He told us that over and over."

"He and this Hampton were in charge?"

"Ian was in charge, but he and Ned Hampton were old friends who'd met in a Texas prison."

"Custis," Trixie blurted out. "I don't know why, but I believe him."

"It doesn't matter."

"Then your mind is made up to kill him?"

"Yes." Longarm started to drag the man back into the stream, but Trixie jumped up and grabbed his arm.

"Get back," Longarm warned. "He might not have actually killed Elizabeth, but he let another man do the job."

"Custis, this is no good. Look, there are people watching."

Longarm turned his head to see a small gathering about fifty yards downstream. They were staring and gesturing.

"Custis, if you drown him, it will be judged a murder. Your old friends will have to come after you. It's not worth it! Elizabeth wouldn't have wanted you to destroy your life. Trust me, I know what I'm saying."

Longarm whirled around. "How could someone like you possibly know what a lady like my Elizabeth would want!"

The moment the words were out, Longarm was overcome with remorse. "Trixie, I'm sorry."

"That's all right. All I meant was that we are both women. Custis, this just isn't right. Turn that piece of scum over to your people. Let a court of law determine if he's telling the truth or not."

"Mister," Reeves pleaded, "listen to her and don't drown me."

"I promised Josh I'd kill every last one of you murdering bastards."

Trixie knelt at his side. "Custis, tell the boy that the law is more important than revenge and that, if you'd carried out your threat, you'd also be a killer."

"All right."

Joe Reeves sobbed with relief.

Longarm hauled the miserable excuse for a man to his feet and shoved him toward the Federal Building. He would turn him over to Billy Vail, and then go looking for Ian and Ned Hampton with or without Billy's blessings.

When Longarm dragged his wet and muddy prisoner into the Federal Building, it was still several hours before most people showed up for work. The guard who manned the night shift took one look at Custis and his man, then said, "Where are you taking him?"

"To a holding cell. Then I'm going to wait for Mr. Vail."

"You don't work here no more. I'm not sure if—"

"Look," Longarm said, trying his best not to run out of patience. "This is one of the men who robbed and murdered the Bonner family and their household staff. Now, you know who I am and that I don't play games. So lock this man in a cell and open up Mr. Vail's office, because it's what he would want you to do."

"Okay," the guard agreed. "Follow me."

They left a trail of muddy footprints as they marched down the empty office corridors. In the back of the building, there was a special set of jail cells where prisoners were held on a temporary basis. Longarm made sure that Joe Reeves was locked up by himself, then followed the guard up to the marshal's office.

The place hadn't changed at all. In fact, Longarm's desk still hadn't been disturbed. He hadn't taken the time to clean it out, and neither had anyone else. He sat down in his battered swivel chair, then motioned Trixie to have a seat.

"Maybe I don't need to be here," Trixie said, looking about nervously. "I mean, I can't tell your ex-boss anything that you don't already know."

"Just relax," Longarm told her as he stared at a wall clock. "Billy is always the first to arrive and the last one to leave. He'll want to ask you some questions."

"Sure," Trixie said. "So what will happen next?"

"I don't know."

"Will he tell you to stop trying to catch Ian and Ned Hampton?"

"He knows I won't."

"So you'll go down to Texas after them?"

Longarm frowned. "They might still be in Denver. Reeves is just guessing. He doesn't really know where they've gone."

"So you believed what he had to say?"

"Yeah, except for the part about not knowing they were going to be killing people. Reeves is no choirboy; he's a hardened criminal."

"How do you know that?"

"I can just tell," Longarm replied. "Also, you told me he was so rough that you wouldn't go back to his room."

"I did say that. But if he doesn't think you believe that he is innocent of murder, then why would he confess?"

"When faced with death, a man will generally buy time any way he can. Even a few minutes becomes very precious."

"Will Reeves hang?"

"He'd damn well better!" Longarm lowered his voice. "Trixie, before Billy gets here, I want to tell you how much I appreciate your help. I came very close to going crazy and drowning Reeves."

"I know."

"I went a little crazy," Longarm admitted. "It hasn't happened very often before. But I've never wanted to kill anyone so much as these men. Elizabeth and her father did not deserve to die. They shouldn't have died. The thieves

113

could have pulled hoods over their heads and robbed the house. They could have left those people bound and gagged and gotten away without anyone being able to identify them later. What they did was savage."

Longarm couldn't say anything more. Trixie hurried over to his side. "You're going to see that justice is done, Custis. It's two down and two to go."

"The worst ones are still free and maybe on their way back to El Paso. They might have taken the Denver and Rio Grande south this morning."

"Even if they did, you will eventually catch them."

Longarm drew a cigar from his pocket. "Smoke?"

"Sure."

He lit her cigar and then one for himself. When Trixie started to talk again, Longarm held up his hand for silence. "Let's settle into silence until Billy arrives. Okay?"

"Whatever you say," Trixie replied, her eyes filled with worry as she blew a cloud of smoke up at the flyspecked ceiling.

Chapter 14

"Custis, you ring-tailed sonofabitch!" Billy Vail shouted as he stormed into the office. "I can't tell you how glad I am to see you again! Why . . ."

The marshal's voice died when he saw Trixie. "Miss, please excuse my swearing. It's just that I wasn't sure that we'd get Custis back again."

"I didn't come here to reclaim my badge," Longarm softly replied. "I brought in one of Elizabeth's killers."

"I know. The guard told me the story." Billy flopped down in an office chair, lacing his fingers behind his head. "Tell me all about it."

"Well, you know about the man I shot and killed yesterday at the pawnshop."

"I had it on my priority agenda to get you in here for questioning today. Was he also one of the men who was at the Bonner Ranch?"

"Yes. He and the fella I brought in this morning were brothers. The one I had to kill was named Wade Reeves. This one is Joe. According to Joe, he and his brother were recruited in El Paso by a big Scot named Ian."

Billy leaned forward looking very intent. "Last name?"

"Reeves said they never learned Ian's last name, and

I'm inclined to believe him. But the fourth man is named Ned Hampton."

"Were all four from El Paso?"

"I have no idea. Ian and Ned Hampton are missing. I don't think that Joe Reeves has any idea where they've gone. He was broke when I grabbed him in a gambling house early this morning."

"The guard says he looks half drowned. Says he is wet and covered with mud, as if he was dragged through a swamp."

"Try Cherry Creek," Trixie said. "Custis decided that Joe needed swimming lessons."

"Yeah," Billy replied cryptically, "I'll just bet. Our friend has some very 'creative' methods of interrogation. I assume you witnessed the one that took place early this morning."

"I did," Trixie told him. "I thought Custis was baptizing the poor bastard."

Billy chuckled, then looked back at his big former deputy marshal. "We've really missed you."

"Any leads on the murders?"

"I'm afraid not. You know that bronze and silver statue of the longhorn that was stolen?"

"Sure. His name was Diablo."

"That's right. Well, we located it in a very expensive gift shop just a few blocks up the street. They said a big Scot brought it in for an appraisal, then offered it for sale. The shop is pretty upset, seeing as they lost their investment."

"They're breaking my heart," Longarm snapped.

"How much money did they get?" Billy asked.

"I forgot to ask Reeves that question."

"Then let's go down and have a little talk with the man." Billy turned to Trixie. "Did you see the other two men?"

"A couple of times. I told Custis about them."

Billy glanced at Longarm, who nodded. "She couldn't tell me anything I didn't already know."

"Fine. Miss, could I have your name and address in case we have some future questions?"

"My name is Trixie and I'm staying at the Embassy Manor."

Billy raised his eyebrows. "That's a pretty expensive hotel."

"I'm . . . I'm on their staff."

"I see," Billy said, clearly not believing the lovely young woman, but satisfied enough with the information.

"Custis?" Trixie asked, preparing to leave. "Will you come back to me?"

"I'm got some things to do here. Then I'll come see you later."

Trixie blew Custis a big kiss and left the two men watching her backside.

"Quite a woman, that one," Billy commented.

"Yes, isn't she, though."

"She seems rather . . . smitten with you."

"Drop it," Longarm growled.

"All right. Let's go down and have a chat with Joe Reeves."

Reeves was shivering on his bunk, trying unsuccessfully to get warm with the aid of a thin woolen blanket. When Longarm and Billy Vail entered his cell, he didn't even bother to sit up.

"This is Marshal Billy Vail," Longarm told the prisoner. "He has some questions for you."

Teeth chattering like dice, Joe Reeves hissed, "I ain't going to say nothing more until I have a lawyer!"

Longarm took three steps forward, grabbed Reeves, and yanked him to his feet. "You'll cooperate if you want to have any chance of being spared a hangman's rope. Now, show this man some respect or by Gawd, I will break your neck like a chicken bone!"

"Custis, let go of that man," Billy ordered, pushing between them and making a big show of protecting Reeves.

Reeves slammed back up against the wall, eyes round with fear. "Mister, that big sonofabitch is determined to kill me!"

"I won't let that happen," Billy promised. "But we have to remember that Marshal Long has been through a lot and he is operating on a very short fuse."

"Keep him away!"

"You're safe now," Billy assured the trembling Texan. "But what he told you is the truth . . . either cooperate or you will surely hang."

Reeves gulped hard. "I told him that it wasn't me or my brother that killed all them people in the rich man's house. It was Ian and Ned Hampton."

"How much money was in Mr. Bonner's safe?"

"I don't know exactly. But it was plenty. You see, Ian and Ned took it out and stuffed it into a pillowcase before anyone had a chance to count. After that, we all took off on horses. My brother and I never got to see the cash being counted, but Ian said it was around five hundred dollars."

Billy scoffed. "It was probably five or ten times that amount."

"It was?"

"That's right. The ranch payroll was in that safe and we estimate that, at a minimum, it would have been at least five thousand dollars."

"Damn! Ian told us that it weren't more than a few hundred."

"Obviously, he lied to you and your brother."

"Yeah, but at least he gave us that old man's horseshoe-shaped diamond ring."

"It was a trick," Billy said, looking contemptuous. "Ian and his partner knew that there was a great danger in attempting to pawn that big diamond ring."

"He knew we'd get caught?"

"He expected it, yes."

Joe Reeves shook his head, looking completely befuddled by this news. "But why would he want that to happen?"

"He mentioned getting on the train south and heading for El Paso, didn't he?"

"Sure, but . . ."

"Well, then, it's obvious. Ian and his friend wanted you to tell us that so we'd believe he was heading for El Paso while he went somewhere else."

Reeves bowed and rested his head in his grimy hands. "To tell you the truth," he muttered, "me and my brother talked about how them two sonsabitches were too smart for us to team up with the first time we met 'em down in El Paso. Wade and I both were afraid we'd get into something way over our heads."

"You were used. Ian must have promised you a lot of money."

"He did. You see, mister, we need it real bad because we needed to pay back rough old Texas boys or we wouldn't never be able to go back home." Reeves lifted his head. "But I swear we never killed nobody. Not before and not out at the Bonner Ranch. And that's the gospel truth."

"Why should we believe you?" Longarm demanded.

"Because we was brought up right by our mother. Sure, we stole chickens and stuff as kids, but we always got a whippin' from Ma. And later, we stole some money and . . . well, a few head of cattle and horses. But I tell you we never would have *killed* anybody."

"I'm inclined to believe you," Billy said, acting sympathetic. "And I'm inclined to put in a good word when you go before a judge who will decide if you will live or get hanged. But you've got to help us every step of the way or I'll not say a word in your behalf."

"You tell me what you want to know and I'll tell you all I can," their prisoner promised. "But I already done told that big bastard standing behind you most everything."

Longarm acted as if he was about to grab the man for

insulting him, and Billy made quite a show of protecting their prisoner.

"Get out of here!" Billy ordered Longarm as if he were enraged by his actions. "I'll speak to you later."

"Fine with me," Custis snapped as he was leaving.

Longarm left the cell knowing that he and Billy had their prisoner right where they wanted him, and that Reeves would do everything in his power to save his own worthless hide. Longarm returned to Billy's office, and was reading the paper when his former boss entered the room.

"You can get your muddy boots off my damned desk!"

Longarm dropped his feet to the floor. "You learn anything more?"

"Only that Ian has a sister and brother-in-law living somewhere up near Cheyenne. Could be that's where he went."

"What about this Ned Hampton fella? Have we got anything on him?"

"I questioned Reeves very closely and didn't learn much. Hampton's the one that wore a black and white cowhide vest. Reeves said he's a professional killer. Says he is quick on the trigger and an expert marksman. Hampton shot down four armed Mexicans and stole their money, saddles, and horses in El Paso. I gather he was anxious to get out of that part of the country before some of the dead men's relatives ambushed him."

"Do you think that the Scot and Hampton have stuck together?"

"Your guess is as good as mine," Billy said.

"So what is our next move?"

Billy reached into his desk drawer and extracted Longarm's badge. "If it's to be *our* move, you're going to have to pin this back on and live up to its standards and oath of office."

"Can you hire me back?"

"I never turned in your termination paperwork," Billy

admitted. "It 'got lost' somewhere in the shuffle. Now, I guess that doesn't matter."

Longarm reached out and plucked one of Billy's ten-cent cigars from a box on his desk. "We've been friends for a lot of years."

"That's right."

"Then I feel obligated to tell you that I'm not too damn sure this is a good idea."

"Why not?"

Longarm put a match to his cigar and inhaled deeply. "Because I'll probably kill Ian and Ned Hampton. In fact, I'm bound and determined to do it."

"I'd like to think that you'd at least try to bring them in alive."

"Sorry."

Billy grabbed a cigar, angrily bit off the end, and jammed it into his mouth before starting to pace back and forth. "Dammit, Custis, I need you on this case, but I can't in good conscience send out a federal executioner."

"Then we have a problem."

"There's *got* to be a solution."

"You're the brains of this outfit. You tell me the answer."

Billy paused in mid-stride, then blew a cloud of smoke into the air. He scowled and looked at Custis. "All right. You have to promise to ask them to drop their guns and surrender to your arrest."

"Not a chance."

"That's the deal. If they don't do it, you have my permission to fill 'em full of lead."

"Billy," Longarm said, coming to his feet, "you just told me that this Ned Hampton is a professional shootist. A hired gun. You know that means he won't just meekly surrender. He'll go for his six-gun while I'm shooting off my mouth askin' him to surrender. And that'll be the death of me."

"I'd suggest you talk very fast."

"Jeezus," Longarm growled. "Some friend you are, putting me in that kind of a predicament. And we don't even know how deadly the Scot is."

"I expect he's every bit as dangerous, probably even more so."

"What if I just walk out of here without the badge?"

"Then I'll send men up to Cheyenne and you'll have complications."

"I don't want to wrangle with any of your boys."

"And they want to even less," Billy told him. "So putting on the badge and promising me that you'll at least ask them to surrender is the less onerous of the two choices you're facing."

"Sounds like."

Billy scooped the badge up and pinned it on Longarm's coat. "Why don't you go and get some rest? I'll send a telegram down to El Paso, just in case we are outsmarting ourselves and they really did head south."

"I'm heading for the train depot," Longarm told him. "A man like the Scot stands out and he might be remembered."

"I can have that little chore handled for you."

"I'd rather do it myself."

"Okay. By tomorrow morning, we should know if they went north or south on the train."

"Either way, I'm heading out after them and I'll need some travel funds."

"I expected that you might," Billy said. "Give me a half hour and I'll have the money."

"Thanks."

"You're welcome," Billy said. "Just like before, huh?"

"No," Longarm told him. "With Elizabeth gone, nothing is like before."

"I'm sorry. Of course it isn't. What about the boy?"

"I'm going to tell him what is going on," Longarm said. "I made the kid a promise that I'll have to go back on and that won't sit well. I guess it can't be helped, though."

"Just get that pair. Alive . . . or dead."

"Count on it."

Less than an hour later, Longarm was talking to the ticket master at the railroad depot. He showed the man his badge, then described the two killers. "The Scot in particular would have stood out."

"Oh, he did, Marshal. I remember him well. He bought a ticket to Cheyenne and told me an off-color joke. Want to hear it?"

"Another time. Was he with the other fella? The one I told you wore a black and white cowhide vest?"

"No, I'm quite certain that he was alone."

Longarm was sorely disappointed. Things would sure have moved to a showdown faster if the two murderers were keeping company.

"I want to buy a ticket for Cheyenne."

"Train leaves tomorrow at noon."

"That's the soonest, huh?"

"You've ridden it enough times to know our inbound and outbound schedule."

"All right."

Longarm paid for his fare and left, intending to go to see Josh and talk things over before returning to the Embassy Manor. But just as he was stepping off the passenger platform, a rifle shot boomed out and a young man walking beside him cried out and dropped like a stone.

People screamed and scattered as Longarm dropped to one knee, drawing his six-gun and searching for the hidden assassin. But the rifleman didn't waste a second shot. He'd vanished.

"Help me!" the man at Longarm's feet pleaded.

Custis looked down to see blood leaking from a bullet wound in the man's side. "We need a doctor. Someone find a doctor!"

While the crowd jumped up, some to escape but others wanting to help, Longarm removed the wounded man's coat, then his shirt. He sighed with relief. "Take it easy. You're going to be all right."

"All right? It hurts!"

"I know, but the bullet passed through and didn't do much more than shatter a rib and cost you some flesh and blood."

"Why me?"

"You weren't the target. I was," Longarm confessed. "We were in a jostling crowd and I got lucky. Sorry about this."

"Dammit anyway. I've only been out West a few weeks. I came from Boston looking for adventure and opportunity, now this. My parents told me not to come out here, but I wouldn't listen. I'm heading back home just as soon as I can . . . providing I don't bleed to death!"

Longarm removed a clean handkerchief from his coat pocket. "Press this up hard against the bullet hole. It will cut down the bleeding. I'm sure that a doctor has been sent for and is on his way."

"Where are you going?" he asked with alarm.

"Looking for whoever shot you," Longarm answered as he hurried off.

"Help!" the young man cried weakly. "Oh, someone get a doctor, please!"

Longarm ran around asking if anyone had seen the shooter, but no one had. Failing that, he hurried across the street, and then made the decision to go and make sure that Josh and Nellie were all right.

When the Scot left, he must have ordered Hampton to stay behind and kill me. And he might also decide to shoot anyone who has seen him.

Chapter 15

When Longarm arrived at Nellie's house, he was relieved to see Josh sitting with the woman on her porch swing.

"Custis!" Josh shouted, jumping off the swing and racing to the picket fence. "We were worried about you."

"And I was worried about *you*," Longarm told the boy as he approached the house. "How have you been?"

"Bored. I want to go home."

"What's the matter, isn't your aunt feeding you right?"

"Why, sure, but I miss the cowboys and all the animals. And I've got work to do helping out."

"Yes, you do," Longarm agreed. "I think that you and your aunt ought to leave for the ranch immediately."

"Whoopee!" Josh shouted.

"What are you talking about?" Nellie asked when Longarm joined her on the swing.

"Two down and two to go," he told her. "I just arrested the brother of the man I killed in that pawnshop."

"You did?" Josh asked with excitement. "Did you kill him slow?"

"I spared his life."

"But you promised you'd—"

"I know," Longarm told the boy, "but I'm convinced

125

that this one really didn't know what was going to happen out at the ranch. I almost drowned him in Cherry Creek. But later I became convinced that he was tricked into thinking that robbery was the only crime he and his brother were supposed to help commit."

Longarm then went on to explain everything that had happened, but he carefully omitted saying anything about either Trixie or the attempted ambush at the train depot. He finished, saying, "So I believe the real pair of killers have fled to Cheyenne. That's why I'm taking the train up there tomorrow."

"But what if that man's story is all a lie?" Nellie asked. "I mean, how can you trust someone like this Joe Reeves?"

"He's facing a hangman unless Billy Vail or an even higher official asks the court to show mercy because of his cooperation. Reeves doesn't want to die, and he's already paid a heavy price. I killed his brother, and he's going to spend a lot of years in prison. Maybe that's enough."

"It isn't," Josh said. "You should have killed him slow like you promised."

Longarm reached out and placed his hands squarely on Josh's shoulders. "If I had done that, I'd have been considered a murderer. I'd have gone to prison for a long, long time. Now, is that what you wanted?"

"No," Josh finally said. "But . . ."

"Josh, I was wrong to promise I'd kill all four men slowly. As for the Scot and the man in the black and white hide vest, I'm going to do everything I can to bring them to justice. I gave my word I'd do that in order to get my badge returned."

"You're a marshal again?" Nellie asked, looking pleased.

Longarm showed them his badge. "It's official. My boss never turned in my resignation. So now I have the authority to do whatever it takes to get those killers and I don't have to worry about going to prison."

"But that means you'll have to try and capture them alive, don't it?" Josh asked.

"Yes," Longarm confessed. "It does. Can you accept that, knowing I'll kill them in a heartbeat if they don't surrender, and if they do surrender, they'll most certainly be hanged?"

"I guess so."

"Good. Nellie, we need to pack up and go to the ranch."

"What's the big hurry?"

"You'll be safer there," Longarm told the woman. "Trust me on this."

"But you said the last of 'em was up in Cheyenne."

"Yeah, but you never know about killers. So I just want to make sure that you're safe before I head up to Wyoming."

"All right," Nellie agreed. "Are you hungry?"

"Do wolves howl?"

"Then come on in and eat. You're still way too skinny."

Longarm followed the little woman into her house, and grinned when he saw a fresh apple pie on her kitchen table. He'd eat, then take them out to Bonner Ranch, and return late this evening in time to spend the night with Trixie before boarding the northbound train.

When Trixie heard the knock on her door, she was so excited to see Longarm again that she unlocked and threw the door open without a thought to her own safety.

"Well, hello there," a handsome man with a warm smile said in greeting. "Are you by any chance expecting Custis Long?"

Trixie frowned. "Why, yes. Who are you?"

"I'm a deputy marshal assigned to the Bonner murder case. I need to talk to Custis, and the sooner the better. We have a lead on the murderers and believe that they are still in Denver."

"But I'm sure they went to El Paso."

"Not so. Unfortunately, they might even be aware that

Custis has made a vendetta out of this case and are planning to kill him."

"Oh, my!"

"Yes." The man nodded. "May I come in?"

"I . . ."

"Our boss, United States Marshal Billy Vail, has asked me to stay here and wait until he returns. Custis *has* to be warned."

"Couldn't you wait downstairs in the lobby?"

"Of course I could! And I will, if you prefer. But what if they came up the back stairs? I'd be down in the lobby and of no help whatsoever. Still, if you feel uncomfortable about me being—"

"No," Trixie said, suddenly feeling quite foolish. "I'm expecting him back any time. It shouldn't take him long to see that Joe Reeves is locked up and then to check on Josh and his aunt."

"Ah, yes, the Bonner boy."

The man took a chair and removed his hat to reveal a full head of wavy hair parted down the middle. Trixie saw that he was fashionably dressed in a tailored brown suit and wore a black derby hat. His shoes were polished to a lustrous shine and his gold watch chain was impressive.

"My name is Matthew Holden."

"Would you like a shot of whiskey?" Trixie asked.

"I can't while I'm on the job. But thanks for the offer."

"I'm going to have one by myself then," Trixie announced. "You know, it's been quite a day. I thought that Custis was going to drown that man this morning. I believe he might have if I hadn't interfered."

"You mean Joe Reeves?"

"That's right. If he hadn't started talking Custis *would* have drowned him in Cherry Creek. But Reeves agreed to cooperate and tell us everything he knows about the terrible Scot and the gunfighter Ned Hampton."

"That's wonderful. You know, I'll never understand

how criminals can rob and then murder their innocent victims."

"They're far worse than just criminals, Marshal Holden. In my view, they're depraved killers. They are rabid dogs that ought to be gunned down on sight!"

"Of course they are!" Holden vigorously agreed. "The hangman's noose is too quick and painless for them. They ought to be . . . well, don't let me get started on how I feel about murderers. Thank heavens the boy wasn't at the house."

"Oh, but he was!" Trixie exclaimed. "You see, Josh was upstairs in his bedroom and saw the four killers leaving on horseback."

"Can he identify them?"

"We expect him to. Josh had a sort of amnesia, but it's all coming back to him. Custis is sure that he'll be able to identify them in a courtroom."

"That's extremely good news."

Trixie frowned. "I'm surprised that you didn't know that, Mr. Holden."

"Matthew. And the reason I don't know the particulars of this case is because I just arrived back from chasing down an outlaw all the way to California. I was expecting a few days off but . . . well, with this crisis, I guess Mr. Vail just figured that I couldn't be spared."

"I see." Trixie poured herself a couple of fingers of whiskey. "Have you known Custis for long?"

"A few years. How about yourself?"

"Only a short time. But I could fall in love with him."

Holden chuckled. "Custis Long is quite a handsome dog, all right. A real ladies' man. When I'm in his company, the women act as if I don't exist."

"Oh, come now," Trixie protested. "I find that difficult to believe."

"It's true." Holden shook his head. "I'm not complaining . . . well, actually I guess I am complaining a bit."

"I take it you are not married."

129

"Never have been. This job just isn't too easy on a marriage."

"Yes, that's what Custis keeps telling me."

"Well, he's being honest," Holden said earnestly. "Bachelor lawmen either get killed, hurt, or grow old and ugly."

"Where are you from?"

"Down south near Pueblo."

"Hmmm." Trixie frowned. "That's kind of odd."

"What do you mean?"

"Where did you get that Texas accent?"

"Ah, that!" Holden shrugged his shoulders. "The truth is, my folks are both from Texas and I was born and raised near San Antonio until I was ten years old. But I've been living in the southern part of Colorado so long that I think of it as my real home. Fact is, I hardly even remember Texas."

"I see." Trixie was about to continue when she was interrupted by a knock on the door. "It must be Custis."

"I'll get it," Holden said, a six-gun appearing in his fist as if my magic.

Marshal Matthew Holden threw open the door, and there stood Hiram Barnaby, resplendent in his expensive suit, hat, and tie with its big diamond stickpin. When he saw Holden, his smile melted and he managed to stammer, "I was expecting Trixie."

"I'm here," she said.

"So I see," Barnaby replied, his expression turning sour. "I was hoping we might have dinner together."

"Some other time."

"Excuse me for mentioning it, Trixie, but you seem," the wealthy man offered, "exceedingly busy of late. Do I need to make an appointment for the evening?"

Trixie blushed. "Mr. Barnaby, let's talk about it tomorrow."

Barnaby stuck out his hand to introduce himself to Holden, and that was when he realized that there was a six-gun pointed at his ponderous belly. He started to retreat, but Holden jammed the pistol in his big gut and hissed, "Come on in, Mr. Barnaby. Are you by any chance Hiram H. Barnaby, the richest banker in eastern Colorado?"

Barnaby's lower lip began to quiver. His eyes sought help from Trixie.

"Well," Holden demanded, voice turning hard and nasty, "why don't you come inside and we can all get better acquainted."

"No, please. I need to . . ."

Holden cocked the hammer of his pistol. "Not another word, Mr. Barnaby. Not if you value your life."

"Hey!" Trixie cried. "What is going on here! Mr. Barnaby doesn't deserve to be—"

"Shut up!" Holden ordered, the back of his hand coming up and striking her in the mouth. He pulled the terrified banker into Trixie's room.

Trixie landed on the floor and tried to say something, but her lips were numb and when she saw the look in Matthew Holden's eyes, she swallowed hard. "You're not a deputy marshal."

"Oh?"

"What's going on here?" Barnaby asked.

"Well," Holden said, "Trixie is right. I'm not a lawman. Quite the opposite, in fact. Now, if you'll both lie face-down on the floor, I'll use that curtain sash to bind you hand and foot."

"Who are you!" Trixie cried.

"I'm the man who is going to kill you both if you don't do as I've asked."

Barnaby hit the floor like a ton of hay, and Trixie was close behind. The man tied them both up and removed Barnaby's wallet, then his watch and rings.

"Not bad," he said. "Four hundred and ten dollars, and the jewelry ought to be worth almost as much. But Trixie, where is your money?"

"I don't have any!"

131

"Oh?"

"Who *are* you!"

"I'm going to gag you both, just in case you might try something really stupid."

Trixie knew better than to struggle, and so did Hiram Barnaby.

"Now," the man said as he stretched out on the bed, "we just wait for Custis Long. When he comes, I'll kill him, then I'll decide if I should also kill both of you. After all, I am a *rabid* dog. Right, Trixie darling?"

When she replied with a muffled oath, he laughed. "Oh, and by the way, Trixie. You were right to be curious about my Texas accent. You see, I come from El Paso and my real name is Ned Hampton."

Chapter 16

Before Longarm climbed back into the rented carriage, he took the Bonner Ranch foreman aside and said quietly, "Now you make sure that those two are never alone. I want someone who can be trusted to shoot fast and shoot straight to be with Josh twenty-four hours a day."

"Don't worry about that," the man assured him. "I won't let him out of my sight. Just get them last two murderin' bastards."

"I will," Longarm vowed.

He said his good-byes to Nellie and the boy, then climbed into the carriage and started back to town. It was late in the afternoon, and Longarm knew that he wouldn't arrive in Denver until well after dark. Trixie would be worried, but that could not be helped. His first obligation had been to see that Josh and Nellie were safe out at the Bonner Ranch, protected by the cowboys.

It was nearly ten o'clock at night when Longarm finally returned the rented horse and carriage to the livery. He was tired and hungry, so he made a quick stop at a little cafe and ordered a large bowl of beef stew. By the time that he reached Trixie's hotel, it was a shade after eleven o'clock.

Longarm trudged wearily across the lobby, and was about to climb the stairs when he was intercepted by one of the hotel clerks, an older man with a worried expression.

"Excuse me, sir?"

Longarm paused, one foot on the landing. "Yes?"

"Would you be here to pay your regards to Miss Trixie?"

Longarm shrugged, seeing no point in denying the fact. "Yes, I am."

"Well, I'm afraid that we might have a small problem in that regard."

"Such as?"

"I've had a few of our other guests visit her room today, but she refuses to answer her door."

"Perhaps she is sleeping."

The clerk gave him a tolerant smile. "Miss Trixie stays up late and she sleeps late, but she always comes down for her meals in our restaurant . . . occasionally with a gentleman, but often alone. Today, I cannot rouse her and she has not appeared."

"Maybe she is off doing other things."

"Do you know Mr. Barnaby?"

Longarm well remembered the rotund and abrasive banker. "Yes, we've met, but I can't say we are friends."

"He is missing. Now I was wondering if . . ."

"Do you worry about *all* your guests this much? Or is it," Longarm continued, "that your employer is annoyed because he is losing a small amount of income from the arrangement between Trixie and this hotel?"

The clerk took a step back. "Sir, I don't discuss my employer's business arrangements. I was merely concerned and thought you might be as well."

"If you were so concerned, then why didn't you use the hotel key and simply open her door?"

"We . . . we lost it."

"Lost it?"

The man's eyes dropped. "Yes, sir."

Longarm shrugged. "I don't have a key either. But if it would put your mind at ease, you can go up there with me. I'm sure that Trixie is asleep."

The clerk looked over his shoulder at the man behind the registration desk, then turned to Longarm and said, "I accept your offer."

"I hope the dear woman isn't ill," the clerk said when they reached the second-floor landing.

"Me too."

Longarm went right up to the door and banged on it loudly. "Trixie, it's Custis! Open up."

But there was no answer, so Longarm pounded on the door even harder. Still no answer.

"She must have gone out," he said with disappointment. "Either that, or someone . . ."

Longarm's thoughts flashed back to earlier in the day when someone had tried to ambush him. He was more worried about retaliation against Josh, but what if Trixie was also a target?

"Mister," he told the clerk. "I'm going to break this door down."

"You can't do that!"

"I'm a United States deputy marshal and Trixie's life may be in danger." Longarm dropped his good shoulder and crashed against the door. But it was solid and well made so that it hardly budged. He reared back and kicked the door with all his might, but it held.

"When all else fails," he said, drawing his gun and aiming it at the doorknob.

"Please don't! You'll alarm every guest in the hotel!"

But Longarm wasn't about to injure his good shoulder, and his leg wound was still sore, so he shouted, "Back off!"

The clerk retreated a dozen steps as Longarm fired twice into the knob, shattering both the handle and the lock. He kicked the door in and dove sideways as someone inside opened fire. Longarm rolled, firing twice as he tried to spot a target, but was blinded by the darkness. He heard movement and started to shoot, but changed his mind. If Trixie were in this room, he might kill her by mistake.

Suddenly, he heard a whispering sound and then a grunt of either pain or exertion, which was followed by two shots so rapid their sound blended. Longarm saw the silhouette of a man dive through Trixie's open window. He heard a body strike the hotel's porch roof below, then the boardwalk. Longarm jumped up and rushed toward the window, but tripped over someone in the darkness.

"Trixie?"

When the person moaned, Longarm reached out and immediately realized it was a man, whom he dragged into the hallway.

"Hiram Barnaby."

The banker's eyes were wide open. Longarm tore away his gag and saw that his lips were covered with frothy red bubbles. Longarm knew the banker was dying, so he rushed back inside the dark room and groped around blindly until he found Trixie. He scooped her up, then carried her out of the room and down the stairs.

In the brightly lit lobby, he could see that she'd been shot in the head but was still breathing. Longarm eased her down on one of the Embassy Manor's expensive blue velvet-covered sofas and tore off her gag, then her ankle and wrist bindings. When the hotel clerk hurried over, Longarm glanced up at the man. "Hiram Barnaby has been shot and is lying in the upstairs hallway. Don't just stand there, go help him!"

Longarm picked Trixie up again and carried her outside, knowing that she'd die if he waited for a doctor. His mind fixed on Dr. Curtis Mason, a newly arrived physician from Chicago, who now lived and practiced medicine only few doors up the street. Hurrying on, Longarm reached the doctor's office, and beat on Mason's door until he appeared blinking like an owl and trying to button up his rumpled nightshirt.

"This woman is hurt bad, Doc!"

"Bring her inside."

They rushed down a hallway into an examination room. A moment later, Mason had the lamps glowing and ordered Longarm to ease Trixie down on an operating table. To his credit, the young doctor didn't waste any time or energy with words. He splashed water onto a bandage and rubbed Trixie's blood-covered forehead wound so vigorously that she cried out, delirious with pain.

"I'm afraid the bullet penetrated her cranium," Mason said, leaning close and probing the bullet hole that entered at her hairline. He rolled her over slightly and examined the back of Trixie's head. "But the slug exited just behind her right ear so she has a chance. Not a good chance, but some chance."

"What can you do?"

Mason straightened. "I'll clean the wound as best I can and hope that we prevent any cranial infection, and I'll attempt to staunch the severe hemorrhaging. Sometimes a damaged brain swells so much that part of the cranium has to be removed to prevent convulsions and death."

"How—"

"You don't need or want to know," Mason told him. "I've never removed part of the cranium, but I've read about it being done successfully."

"But Doc—"

"Marshal, this young woman's chances of survival are, at best, fifty-fifty. I'll do what I can, and the only thing left for you is to pray."

Longarm felt devastated by the news he'd just heard, and muttered, "God doesn't listen to me, Doc. At least not very damn often."

"He listens to everyone, Marshal. Why don't you wait outside."

"There is another shooting victim at the Embassy

Manor, but he was hit in the chest and was breathing bloody bubbles when I left."

"Then he's a dead man," the doctor said. "You brought the correct victim to me, and I'll do my best to save her life."

"Doc, whatever it costs, I'll pay."

"Get out of here," Manson told him. "Come back in the morning."

"I . . . I don't think I can."

The physician glanced up at Longarm, eyes questioning, but Longarm didn't have time to explain. He ran all the way back to the hotel. By now, they had brought Hiram Barnaby downstairs and laid the prominent banker out in the lobby, then covered him with a silk sheet. Several guests and hotel staff stood around the man's body.

Longarm dashed upstairs to Trixie's room, found nothing that would help him to find or identify the killer, then hurried back outside. After a moment of deliberation, he deduced the exact place where the gunman must have landed after throwing himself out of Trixie's window.

"Hey," Longarm shouted to one of the curiosity-seekers holding a lantern. "Bring that light over here!"

Longarm snatched the kerosene lamp from the man and began to scour the area for evidence. He didn't have to look very hard to discover fresh bloodstains spattering the sidewalk.

"Did anyone see who fell out of the upstairs window and struck the porch before landing here?" he asked the half-dozen onlookers.

They all said no.

Longarm unholstered his gun and raised the lantern, saying, "Why don't you people all go back to bed or your entertainment."

"What about my lantern!"

Longarm didn't even bother to reply as he started to follow the trail of blood down the sidewalk north toward the main business district and the Federal Building. It was a part of Denver that fell empty and silent by early evening. A part of town where people came to work, then immediately left for home. There were vagrants and a few drunks that entered this deserted section of town to sleep until morning. There were even a few cutthroats and thieves who found the area profitable.

But Longarm didn't care about any of them as he marched down the street with a lantern in his left hand and his gun clenched in his right hand. He was on the trail of the notorious and mysterious Ned Hampton, a man who had shot two more innocent victims without a moment's hesitation or thought of mercy. A man said to be lightning quick with a gun and an expert marksman.

Hampton is either shot or has torn himself up in that bad fall out of Trixie's window. He may be broken up inside or bleeding to death, but as long as he still moves and breathes, he's a killer needing to be out of his misery.

Chapter 17

The blood-drippings took Longarm through the business part of town, and then onto Nellie Bass's quiet residential street. That told Longarm that Ned Hampton was out to kill Josh, but was unaware that the boy had just gone out to the Bonner Ranch. As Longarm limped down the dark and quiet street toward Nellie's house, he could see that it was the only one that was brightly lighted.

Longarm ducked down behind Nellie's picket fence, shielded from the house by Nellie's roses. Reloading his spent cartridges, he watched the house for a few minutes just in case Hampton was still inside. But nothing moved inside, so Longarm crept up to the front porch, then put his hand on the doorknob and jumped inside, crouched and ready to fire.

The house was empty, but Ned Hampton had been there only minutes earlier. Longarm tracked the killer's fresh bloodstains through one room after another. Hampton had found bandages and had apparently doctored his wounds, managing to stop the bleeding. The trail ended on Nellie's back porch, and that was where Longarm sat down trying to decide what to do next. There was no doubt in his mind that Hampton was still in this quiet neighborhood, but he might be hiding in any one of dozens of yards.

"If I were Ned Hampton, what would I do?" he asked himself out loud as he tried to put himself in the desperate fugitive's position.

"I'd want to leave this part of the country, but I'd also want to be sure that there were no possible witnesses. And who else might have seen me, other than Josh? I'd think that Trixie and the banker were dead . . . because I'd shot them nearly point-blank in that upstairs hotel room. No one other than Josh could possibly tie me to the Bonner Ranch murders."

Longarm stood and looked up at the stars. In only a few short hours, night would begin to turn into day. "If I were physically able, I'd try to kill that boy before I ran because, with Josh Bonner dead, I'd never have to worry about being tied to the murders."

Hampton is going to make one last attempt at killing Josh.

That was Longarm's conclusion, and even if he were wrong and Hampton's only thought was of escape, at least Josh would remain safe. Longarm knew that he had to get out to the Bonner Ranch before Hampton, and make doubly sure that Josh stayed inside and therefore could not possibly be ambushed by an expert rifleman.

Twenty minutes later, he was waking up Earl Payson, the livery owner, and asking the sleepy man to saddle him a fast horse.

"Can't it wait until morning?" Payson complained. "Man, I'm forty-seven years old and I need some rest."

"I'm sorry," Longarm told the man. "But a young boy's life may be at stake."

Payson rolled out of bed, knuckled his eyes, and said, "In that case, we're wasting time jawing."

"Thanks Earl."

Ten minutes later, Longarm was climbing stiffly into the saddle and galloping northwest out of Denver. He sure hoped that he would get there before Ned Hampton.

Maybe I'm wrong and he's headed for Cheyenne to join the Scot. How long will it take me to pick up their cold trail if that happens?

Longarm rode as hard as he dared toward the Bonner Ranch, eyes straining ahead in case he overtook the wounded Ned Hampton. It was a dark, cloudy night and there were few stars out, making it very difficult to see well. Fortunately, Longarm followed a wide and well-traveled road. When he finally arrived at the ranch, the sound of his mount's hoofbeats brought cowboys pouring out of the bunkhouse with their guns drawn.

"Where is Josh!" Longarm shouted.

"He's upstairs," Sanders replied, stepping out of the house with a shotgun in his hands.

"Good," Longarm said, relaxing in the saddle. He waited until the other cowboys gathered around, and said, "One of the killers is named Ned Hampton. He's hurt, but I don't know how badly. I tracked him to Miss Bass's house, but then he vanished. He's after Josh and he's an expert marksman."

"He won't get within a mile of here without us seeing him first," a cowboy vowed.

Josh and Nellie appeared, and Longarm had to repeat what had happened upstairs at the Embassy Manor. "I'm afraid that Hampton killed a banker named Hiram Barnaby and he shot Trixie in the head."

"Is she dead?" the boy asked.

"No. I got her to a doctor and he said she might pull through. I went after Hampton, but he escaped. I figure he's on his way out here for you, Josh."

"I hope so," Josh replied, chin lifting. "If he does come here, we can finally kill him."

Longarm dismounted. "We'd better all go back into the house. Someone put this horse away quick. Then the rest of you go back to the bunkhouse and turn off your lamps. If Hampton is coming to kill Josh, I want him to think that everyone is sleeping."

"Custis, I want you to know that I don't approve of this game," Nellie groused. "You're asking us to be his *bait*."

"Sooner or later," Longarm told the woman, "Ned Hampton must be stopped. Let's hope it's before daybreak. With luck, I can take him alive and he'll lead us to the Scot."

"What do you want me to do?" Grant Sanders asked.

"Position yourself near the back door. Don't forget, Hampton knows the layout of this house."

"Should I try and wing him or shoot him dead?"

"If you have time, aim for a leg," Longarm replied. "I need him to lead me to the Scot."

"If our man comes sneaking up to the back door, I'll blow a hole in his kneecap," Sanders promised.

"Just don't take any chances," Longarm warned. "Hampton is a professional gunfighter and it's clear that he'll shoot fast and straight."

"I'll keep that in mind," Sanders vowed as he moved off around the house.

Nellie and Josh were too nervous to sleep, and the boy wanted to stay downstairs, but Longarm made him go up to his room. "Do you have a gun up there with you?"

Josh nodded. "I didn't used to, but now I sleep with one of Grandpa's pistols."

"Just be careful you don't shoot me if you hear trouble downstairs."

When Josh and Nellie went up to their rooms, Longarm turned off all the downstairs lights. Then he took a seat in the parlor and waited to see if the trap he'd set would soon be sprung.

A rooster crowed just before the dawn, and a dozing Longarm jumped out of his chair. He was tired and sore, but if Hampton were to make his move, he'd have to do it very soon. Longarm moved to the front window and peered out through the curtains. He saw nothing, which was expected, and he found himself debating whether or not to go outside and then around in back to make sure that Grant Sanders was still awake and alert.

"I hope he's holding out better'n I am," he muttered, disgusted with himself.

Afraid of dozing off again, Longarm began to silently pace back and forth. There was a huge grandfather clock in the hallway, and its pendulum made a slight ticking sound as it swung back and forth. Longarm soon discovered that he was listening to the clock instead of approaching danger. He decided that he really needed to go outside and check on how the ranch foreman was doing. If Hampton tried to get inside this house, he'd most likely come in from the back and then through the big kitchen.

Longarm tiptoed silently past the noisy clock and into the kitchen. He crossed the floor, then angled sharply to the right past a pantry and then out onto the back porch.

"Sanders!" he whispered into the darkness.

"Yeah?" the foreman hissed.

"You okay?"

There was a pause, then: "I'm having trouble staying awake."

"Me too," Longarm admitted, eyes straining to locate the voice. "Hear anything?"

"Nope. Could you spell me a minute?"

Longarm eased open the porch's screen door and took a step down on the rickety wooden stairs. "Where the hell are you?"

"Right here," a voice tensely grated.

Longarm knew in less than a heartbeat that Grant Sanders was a dead man and that he was about to join him. Hampton didn't risk a gunshot, but instead hurled a knife, which struck Longarm as he was twisting sideways to jump back into the house. The throwing knife deflected off his gold-plate pocket watch, then pierced his flesh just under the rib cage. Longarm caught his boot heel on the top step and tripped, falling hard on the stairs. He tried to tear his gun free, but it was pinned between himself and the steps. By then, Hampton was on him like a big cat.

Longarm knew that he'd already have been shot if it hadn't been that Hampton required silence in order to kill Josh and escape. And now, with the professional's knife sawing at his side, Longarm tried to throw Hampton back to give himself some reaching room.

But the killer hit him with an overhand right that caused the back of Longarm's skull to strike the door frame, nearly rendering him unconscious. Hampton hit him again, and Longarm felt himself losing consciousness. In desperation, he tried to shout a warning, but Hampton reared back and launched a vicious kick at his face. Longarm felt the man's boot graze his chin, and he managed to grab it coming back down. With what little remained of his strength, Longarm threw his arms overhead, and Hampton struck the ground so hard the air exploded from his lungs.

They were both gasping and out of breath, each striving with all his might to kill the other quickly. Hampton rolled sideways, barely avoiding Longarm's knees, which came down with enough force to have crushed his chest. Longarm threw a hurried punch, and felt his knuckles collapse the killer's nose. Hampton grunted in pain and lunged forward, thumbs seeking Longarm's eye sockets.

They locked and rolled over and over in the backyard. Hampton was the smaller man, but he was extremely quick and powerful. Longarm shouted, and the lights in the upstairs bedroom blazed as Josh threw open his window and raised a lamp, which cast an eerie yellow glow on the two men bent on killing each other.

Longarm looped a sledgehammerlike overhead that connected again against Hampton's nose, and the man fell back, howling. Longarm followed that up by diving on the murderer and using both hands on his neck, trying to throttle him to death. Hampton slammed his knee up between them and bowled Longarm over backward. When Longarm crawled to his feet, the killer scooped up a handful of dirt and threw it in Longarm's eyes. Momentarily blinded, he had no choice but to draw his pistol and open fire.

Hampton tackled him and they each fought to gain the upper hand. The killer landed a short, chopping blow to Longarm's jaw, and then tore at the gun in his fist. Longarm butted Hampton in the face, and Hampton tried again to get a thumb in his eyes. Longarm found himself on the bottom, covered with the blood that was pouring from Hampton's broken nose and lips. The clouds slipped away for a moment, and he could see the pure hatred stamped on the killer's ghoulish face.

A pistol shattered the darkness and Hampton reared back, mouth wide open as he gazed up at the boy holding a gun. Josh fired again, and Hampton raised his arms and then sighed as he fell backward.

"Stop!" Longarm bellowed, rolling away from the killer, who was still trying to attack him.

But Josh kept firing until his grandfather's pistol was empty and Ned Hampton was no longer even quivering. Then the gun slipped from the boy's fingers and he disappeared, only to reappear a few moments later. Josh ran up the dead man and kicked him hard in the side of the face.

"I'd piss on him," he chocked, "if Aunt Nellie wasn't coming down here to see it."

Longarm struggled to his feet. He was shaky, and his ears were ringing like a blacksmith's anvil. Ned Hampton wasn't going to be any help in finding the Scot now, but on the other hand, he wasn't ever going to kill again.

"Come inside," Nellie said.

"Not until we find Grant Sanders," Longarm whispered.

A few moments later, the cowboys burst around the corner of the house with drawn guns and lanterns.

"It's over!" Longarm yelled, throwing up his arms. "Don't shoot!"

"Oh, sweet Jeezus," a cowboy whispered. "It's Sanders. His . . . his throat's been cut from ear to ear."

Josh sobbed, and started kicking his mother's murderer

with rage. Nellie grabbed the boy, and Longarm helped her to drag him back into the house.

"Josh, it's done!" Longarm said, crushing the boy to himself. "Ned Hampton is finally dead."

"There's still one left!"

"I'll find and kill him before this day is over," Longarm vowed. "Just . . . just take it easy and let go."

Josh began to cry as hard as ever a boy cried. Longarm held him close and looked up at Nellie, whose expression was bleak.

"He's going to be all right," Longarm promised. "When I get the Scot, he'll finally be all right."

The older woman shook her head and then shuffled into the kitchen, maybe to pour everyone a drink, but probably to make a strong pot of coffee.

Chapter 18

Longarm had bathed and shaved. Because his own clothes were torn and bloodstained, at Nellie's suggestion he'd rummaged through old Clyde Bonner's bedroom closet. It was there that he selected a very fine suit, shirt, and polished pair of boots that were all a shade too tight but would do for his trip to Cheyenne. The rancher's hat size was also a mite too small, but Longarm put his knee into a cream-colored Stetson and stretched it so hard that it settled right down to his ears. The hat alone was probably worth a month of his federal wages.

Now, the sun was well off the eastern horizon and it was time to leave the ranch and return to town. The Denver and Rio Grande pulled out at noon, and it was Longarm's sworn intention to be on that train and hunting the Scot the moment his new boots landed in Wyoming. If he really got lucky, the Scot would be waiting at the train depot in the expectation of seeing Ned Hampton.

Hampton. When Longarm thought about their fight to the death only a few hours earlier, he had to shake his head. Despite having several deep gashes on his body from falling out of the hotel, Hampton had almost killed him. Probably would have killed him if it hadn't been for Josh taking a highly risky shot and drilling the man.

I need rest and recuperation. I haven't been so run-down and underweight since the war. When this is over, I'm taking a month off and doing nothing except eating and sleeping.

The cowboys were waiting for Longarm as he stood on the front porch in his expensive clothes, trying to think of something that would make Josh feel better. But there wasn't much of anything he could say, so Longarm just gave the kid a hug and said, "You saved my life this morning. He would have killed me."

"Naw. You'd have gotten on top and finished him," Josh said. "But I thought you needed a little help."

"I'm glad you're a good shot with that pistol."

"Grandpa and I used to go out and shoot at targets. I've shot that one so many times I could blow the head off a flying hornet."

"Josh, don't worry about me. I'll get the Scot."

"I know you will."

Longarm kissed Nellie on the cheek, and climbed into a buckboard that one of the cowboys was going to drive to Denver. He waved at the solemn group and as they rolled out of the ranch yard, his thoughts turned to Trixie. Was she still fighting for life, feeling better, or just dead? Poor Trixie and that pompous ass Hiram Barnaby had done nothing except to be in the wrong place at the wrong time. Barnaby had paid for that mistake with his life.

Longarm was so lost in his dark thoughts that the driver's voice startled him. "Marshal Long, my name is Luke. I sure am sorry about all this killin', but I want you to know that I'm going to Cheyenne with you this afternoon."

"Thanks," Longarm said, really noticing the tall, handsome young cowboy for the first time. "I appreciate your offer, but I work best alone."

"I'm sure that is true, but I have more than a little interest in helping you finish this deal up with them killers.

You see, Mr. Bonner gave me a job as a cowboy when no one else would give me a chance. I'd been in some bad scrapes as a kid and arrested once or twice, I'm sorely ashamed to say."

"We all make mistakes, Luke."

"Yeah, but I was sent to prison when I was sixteen for robbing a bank."

"That's a serious mistake."

"It was. Fortunately, no one was hurt but me. I didn't get very far before I was caught in a little Nebraska farm town. The people up there were upset enough to hang me, but the town marshal said that would be breaking the law as much as I'd broke the law by robbin' the bank."

"That marshal was correct."

"Yep. And he saved my sorry hide. I'd have been a goner if it hadn't been for that Nebraska marshal. And after I got out of prison, I rode back up to Nebraska to thank the man, but he'd been killed in a shoot-out. His name was Johnson. Ruben Johnson. You ever hear of him?"

"I'm afraid not."

"He reminds me of you. Same big size and toughness. But he was fair and went by the book. Just like yourself."

"I've been known to bend the law a time to two myself, Luke. I'm probably gonna bend it when I finally catch up to the Scot."

"Excuse me for being so bold, but I think that would be a mistake. Also, I am convinced that you need some help on account of how beat up you are right now."

Longarm stared straight ahead. "Luke, how old are you?"

"I'll turn twenty-two next July."

"The Scot is smart and ruthless. He just might prove to be one of the most dangerous killers I've ever hunted. A few hours ago, I asked your foreman, Grant Sanders, to guard the back of the house. He did his best and for that, he got his throat cut. Do you hear what I'm trying to tell you?"

"Sure. You're saying that the same thing could happen to me. But after a man has done a few years in prison, he learns how to take care of himself. Grant Sanders was a fine man to work for, but he wasn't much with a gun."

"I doubt you are either."

"That's true enough, I suppose," Luke said. "But I wasn't a cowboy either when Mr. Bonner overlooked my past mistakes and hired me on at full wages. He gave me a chance and I'd like to pay him back. The only way I can do that is by helping you to get the last one of the bunch that murdered him and Miss Bonner."

"I'm sorry, but the answer is still no."

Luke sighed. "Then I guess that I just quit my job for nothin'. I told Josh what I was going to do and he gave me his blessings."

"All the more reason why you should drop me off at the Embassy Hotel and then head on back to the ranch."

Luke drove along in silence for a bit, then said, "Marshal, I can see how you'd think that. But the truth is, I've *got* to help you whether you want my help or not. I'm damn sure no hero. But I do owe Mr. Bonner and Johnson. I've often thought that if I hadn't been penned up in prison, maybe I'd have gone to live in that Nebraska town. And who knows?"

"What?"

"Maybe I'd have been there and saved Marshal Johnson's life. Or failing that, I'd have been at the ranch when this bunch arrived and I'd have been able to save their lives too."

Longarm took a deep breath. "Sounds to me like you're feeling guilty about something that you couldn't have prevented. Guilt is a bad thing, Luke. It eats at a person as if they'd swallowed poison. I don't believe much good comes from guilt, and I've known people whose entire lives have been ruined because of feeling bad about something they should have or should not have done."

"Marshal, what you say is right, up to a point. But guilt

151

also forces a man to right some of his wrongs in addition to trying to be a better person."

Longarm could see that he just wasn't getting through to this earnest young cowboy. "Do you remember how many mistakes you made when you first tried to become a cowboy?"

"Shoot, yes!" Luke managed a grin. "I couldn't rope for beans. I wasn't much good on a horse and didn't know one end of a longhorn from the other. I don't know how Mr. Sanders and the boys put up with me, and I sure didn't earn my wages that first year."

"But I'll bet you're good now."

"I don't mean to brag," Luke said, "but now I am one of the best. Fact is, there is no one better when it comes to breaking young horses."

"I believe you. But the point I was making is that you made a lot of mistakes when you were learning. I'm sure some of those mistakes got you banged up pretty good. But with a killer like the Scot, even a tiny mistake will get you dead. I can't let that happen."

"Fair enough," Luke said. "But you also can't stop me from trying to help."

Longarm's brow furrowed. "Tell me something, cowboy. Have you always been this stubborn, or is it something you picked up in prison?"

"I was always stubborn. Mr. Bonner used to talk with me when I was pretty discouraged about becoming a cowboy. He told me that if a man wanted something, he had to go at it hard and never quit. He said a lot of people have dreams and ambitions, but damn few are willing to do the tough work it takes to make 'em come true."

"Mr. Bonner was right."

"I think so too," Luke agreed. "And now I want to become a law officer like you and Mr. Johnson."

"Take my advice and stick to being a first-rate cowboy."

"No, sir, I just can't do that anymore. I loved the life

and the challenges, but now I want to try something tougher."

"Cowboying is as tough as it gets."

"True," Luke admitted. "But it has gotten just a shade common to me now, and that's a fact that I'm ashamed to admit."

"Luke . . ."

"I'm going to Cheyenne. I drew my wages and am payin' my own way to Wyoming. I would like to be at your side tracking down a murderer, but I'll settle for being on the outside if that's the way things have to be between us."

Longarm could read men well, and he could see that this cowboy wasn't going to be talked out of his decision. That being the case, there was no point in further argument or discussion. "You win, Luke. But I'll take no responsibility if you get killed. I'm already feeling bad about Miss Trixie and your brave foreman. I let them down and I've made too many mistakes."

"Maybe you have and maybe you haven't," Luke replied. "All I know is that thanks to you, three of the four men who murdered my boss and his daughter and household staff are either dead or in jail."

Longarm just shook his head.

"What's the matter?" asked Luke. "Did I say something wrong?"

"No, it just occurred to me that you really ought to remain a working cowboy because of the way you sling the bullshit."

Luke chuckled softly, then grew serious and patted the six-gun on his hip. "If you think I sling bullshit good, just wait until you see the way I sling hot lead."

"Oh? Stop this buggy up and let's see if your aim is as good as your talk, cowboy."

"Right now?"

"Better now than later."

Luke reined in their horses and set the brake. They were

out in the open with only a few bushes and trees, so he drew his gun, looked in all directions, and said, "Marshal, darned if I see a target."

"How about that black rock up ahead?"

"What rock?"

Longarm pointed. "The one by the road."

Luke squinted. "Why, it ain't no bigger than a horny toad!"

"Shoot at it anyway," Longarm commanded.

Luke drew his gun, raised it, and took careful aim. When he fired, their horses jumped and the carriage skidded forward. Luke's shot was far wide to the left.

"Try again," Longarm told the cowboy. "Empty your gun and let's see how many times you manage to come close."

Luke fired four more rounds, and his best shot was a good two feet away. Longarm drew his own pistol, and without raising it to eye level, fired from the waist. His shots came one upon the other and the rock jumped four times out of five attempts.

"Holy cow!" Luke exclaimed. "Now *that* is some kind of sharpshooting!"

"You're good breaking broncs, I'm good with a gun."

"A damn sight better than good, I'd call it."

"Thanks," Longarm replied. "But the fact is, Ned Hampton was every bit as good as I am and maybe even a hair better. That's the way it is when you are a professional. I couldn't ride a bucking horse nearly as well as you, and you can't shoot fast or straight enough to save my hide in a pinch."

"I'm much better with a rifle."

"Most men are."

Luke flicked the lines and the horses broke into a trot. "Marshal Long, either way, I'm bound for Cheyenne. You can't arrest me unless I do something against the law."

"I could," Longarm told the square-jawed young cowboy, "but I won't."

154

"Good," Luke replied. "So let's not be talking about what could go wrong, and instead be thinking about what we need to do right. Mr. Bonner taught me that lesson, and it has served me well."

"You got the makings for a smoke?" Longarm asked. "I ran out of cigars."

"I do."

Longarm was not accustomed to rolling his own cigarettes, and the tobacco that Luke carried was a cheap, noxious weed that hardly passed for being tobacco. But he rolled one for himself, then held the lines while Luke rolled a far better cigarette for himself. Then, with nothing much more to talk about, they smoked in silence on their way back to Denver.

When Longarm burst into Dr. Mason's office, the first thing he saw was Trixie sitting in a chair with her head swathed in bandages. Her face was puffy and bruised, but she was smiling.

"Boy, are you a sight for sore eyes!" Longarm exclaimed, rushing forward to give the lovely young woman a hug. "When I brought you here last night, you were in bad shape."

"I don't remember a thing until this morning."

Dr. Mason entered the room. "Ah, Marshal Long. So you've come to see our miracle girl."

Longarm stepped back and stared. "Trixie, I can't believe how good you look after last night."

"I wish I could say the same thing about you," Trixie told him. "Did you find and kill that horrible man?"

"Yes. He came out to the Bonner Ranch to kill young Josh. We managed to stop him, but not before he killed a good cowboy."

"Mr. Barnaby is dead."

"I know." Longarm turned around, saw Luke holding his hat in his hands, and said, "Trixie. Dr. Mason. This is

Luke. He and I will soon be leaving on the train for Cheyenne."

Luke surprised Longarm with his sudden shyness. The tall cowboy gulped. "Honored to make your acquaintance, Miss Trixie."

"Me too."

"Dr. Mason," Luke said, "do you remember me? I'm the fella that landed on his arm a few months back after getting tossed by a bronc. You set the bone and it's healed just fine."

"Yes, I remember you now. They said you were the best bronc buster on the Bonner Ranch, or for that matter, any ranch in Colorado."

"Every cowboy meets his match now and then," Luke said modestly. "But I sure do thank you for setting my arm for only ten dollars."

"You're welcome, Luke."

Trixie frowned. "Custis, are you sure this cowboy is gonna be helpful in Cheyenne? He looks pretty green."

Before Longarm could answer that question, Luke said, "Miss, I'm a tough hombre, despite my gentle good looks."

"Modest, ain't he?" Trixie said with a half smile.

"Thank you, miss. I promise I'll be more help than hindrance to the marshal. He and I have already talked the whole thing over."

"Luke," Custis told the doctor and Trixie, "has shown himself to be more stubborn than any mule. I tried to talk him into staying a Colorado cowboy."

"And you might have succeeded, Marshal, if you'd have told me about Miss Trixie."

Longarm shook his head. "He's also a real charmer. Luke, why don't you go buy some bullets or something?"

"I got enough already."

"Then find something else to buy."

"Yes, sir. I can tell when I'm not wanted." He tipped his hat to Trixie and left the doctor's office.

"He's sure a cocky sort," Trixie said. "Handsome as anything, but full of himself."

"Luke is a good man," Longarm told her. "And he might even prove useful to me in the days or weeks to come. How did you make such a fast recovery?"

"Ask Dr. Mason. All I know is that I woke up late this morning with this terrible headache and awful bandage."

When Longarm turned his attention to the doctor, Mason shrugged his shoulders and said, "Who knows what the brain can tolerate or how it will respond to a less than lethal injury? There have actually been people who have had arrows shot into their brains, and bullets, and survived in good health. So I can't answer your question, Marshal Long. All I can say is that your prayers must have helped."

"I . . . uh . . ."

"Thanks to both of you," Trixie told them. "I'm going back to the Embassy Manor and sleep for a few days. I'm sure tired. Custis, thank heavens you killed that horrible Ned Hampton. He sure had me fooled when he first came to my door. He said his name was Marshal Matthew Holden and he seemed to know all about you and the other federal lawmen."

"He must have had a friend working at the Federal Building," Longarm replied.

"Would you take me back to the hotel now?" Trixie asked.

"Sure."

Longarm escorted Trixie to her hotel room, which had been cleaned and straightened. "Are you going to be all right here after what happened?"

"Of course." Trixie held him close for a moment. "Just come back safe and bring that handsome cowboy with you."

"Does he interest you?" Longarm asked, hearing the shrill blasts of the train whistle telling him that it would soon be departing the depot for Cheyenne.

"All good-looking bachelors interest me." Trixie looked up at him. "When I lost consciousness, I dreamed wonderful dreams, Custis. You want to know what I dreamed?"

"I don't have much time before the train leaves."

"I dreamed I was married and had three beautiful children. And we all went to church every Sunday and I was very respectable."

"That is a nice dream."

"Could you ever get married and have children with a woman like me?"

"Trixie, I just lost the woman that I thought I'd marry and spend the rest of my life loving. I can't answer your question."

"I didn't think you could . . . or would," Trixie said, trying to hide her obvious disappointment. "But that's all right. Maybe I'll ask you again sometime . . . if I don't find another tall, handsome man eager to tie the knot and be a good father to his children."

Longarm smiled, kissed her on the cheek, and left before he got into big trouble.

When he arrived at the depot, the train was loaded and the conductor was jumping on board. Longarm had to run to catch the caboose and jump on board. He sat down and caught his breath, wondering if Luke was in one of the coaches up ahead or if he'd perhaps changed his mind and decided to remain in Denver.

No, he wouldn't change his mind. He's up front waiting for me. He'd go to Cheyenne and try to find the Scot, even if he had to do it alone.

"Hey!" Luke shouted, bursting into the caboose and looking peeved. "You damn near didn't make it!"

"Ah, but I *did* make it."

"Well, I sure hope you don't act like that all the time."

Longarm didn't even bother to respond. Instead, he stretched out on a bench, pulled Clyde Bonner's fine Stetson down over his eyes, and fell asleep. There were 106 miles of track separating Denver from Cheyenne, and it was Longarm's full intention to sleep away at least a hundred of them.

Chapter 19

Custis stepped off the train in Cheyenne and heard his name being called. He turned to see a boy of about fifteen years old hurrying across the passenger platform waving a telegram.

"Sir," the boy said breathlessly, "I was paid a dollar just to make sure that you got this the minute you arrived!"

"How'd you know who I was?"

"The telegram said you were tall and beat-up-looking, probably with a limp." The kid grinned, showing prominent buck teeth. "You're the tallest and ugliest fella that just got off the train, so it was easy enough to figure."

"Thanks," Longarm said cryptically as he collected the telegram and started to read.

"Uh-hem," the boy said. "Uh-hem!"

Longarm looked up from the telegram to see the kid with his hand stuck out. "Hey, you already got paid a dollar," Longarm said.

"But it's customary to be paid at *both* ends."

"You're a little thief," Longarm groused as he handed the boy a nickel.

"And you're awful cheap," the kid said an instant before he darted away.

"News already?" Luke asked, trying to hide his amusement.

"It appears so."

"Well, are you going to let me in on that important news . . . or not?"

Longarm's brows knitted. "It's from my boss. Marshal Billy Vail. He telegraphed to say that Joe Reeves, the only one of the bunch that I've managed to take alive so far, has done some more talking." Longarm read the telegram aloud:

REEVES SUDDENLY REMEMBERED SCOT'S LAST NAME MCFAIN **STOP** ALSO REMEMBERED IAN MCFAIN HAS SMALL CATTLE RANCH ABOUT TEN MILES NORTH OF CHEYENNE CALLED BAR M **STOP** SAID MCFAIN HAS LOTS OF FAMILY AND FRIENDS **STOP** CUSTIS BE CAREFUL

"That's it, huh?" said Luke.

"That's it," Longarm replied.

"So we head for the ranch tonight?"

"Nope." Longarm stifled a yawn. "We'd best get a room and some sleep. Tomorrow morning, we have a good breakfast, ask some questions about Ian McFain, and try to figure out exactly what we are up against. Then we plan our move against the Scot."

"I don't see why we don't ride up to the Bar M tonight and try to take the murderin' sonofabitch by surprise."

"I'll put it to you real simple, Luke. If you walk into a trap or a situation where you are badly outgunned, then it's doubtful you'll get to *deliver* your prisoner to the authorities . . . much less live to collect your next paycheck. Understand?"

The cowboy blushed. "Sure. I just ain't one to sit around when the prize is at hand. I like to jump right into things."

"Then you'll likely never live long should you take up the life of a lawman," Custis warned. "I like to stay at the

Antelope Hotel. The rooms are clean, the sheets are fresh, and the price is right."

"Whatever you say. I've never been up here before. This town is a whole lot busier than I'd expected."

"Cheyenne is a major railhead. It's also one of the largest repair shops where the Union Pacific works on their big locomotives. Add that to the fact that it is surrounded by some of the best grassland in the West and biggest ranches, and you can see why it has prospered."

"Wyoming cowboys think they're real special, and I don't care for 'em all that much," Luke said. "They'll come down to Denver and try to hoo-rah the whole damn town. Get into some terrible fights, and most always get whipped down to a nubbin. I've loaded more than a few on this train and sent 'em home with knots all over their dumb heads. They can't break broncs all that good either."

"Sure, sure," Longarm responded. "Let's stop by the marshal's office and tell him we're here on business."

"What for? We don't need him."

"We do if he says we do."

"That's how it works, huh?"

"That's right," Longarm told the kid. "It's called 'professional courtesy.' A town marshal doesn't like to learn secondhand that another lawman is in his jurisdiction on official business."

"His what?"

"Jurisdiction," Longarm repeated as they started walking up the street toward the hotel. "It means his legal area of responsibility."

"Why would he care?"

"Well, let's suppose you were the town marshal here. Would you appreciate it if other lawmen came in and started throwing their weight around?"

"I suppose not."

"Then you can understand the situation," Longarm said.

"Marshal Ezra Foster is a good man. He can probably tell us plenty about Ian McFain."

"Whatever you say. I'm just up here to help out any way I can."

"Sure," Longarm growled.

When they stepped into Foster's office, the marshal was dozing in his office chair with his boots resting on his cluttered desk. The marshal of Cheyenne was now well into his sixties, and Longarm knew he was still tough and capable. Foster had been a real town-tamer in his younger days, and was still highly respected by Cheyenne's rougher element, as were his two deputies.

"Marshal Foster," Longarm said rather loudly as he bumped the man's chair, "how are you doing these days?"

"Well, if it isn't Deputy Marshal Custis Long!" Foster exclaimed, acting as if he'd been awake all the time. "Boy, you look like you've been wrestlin' wildcats! You need to put on the feed bag, son."

"I mean to as soon as I take care of the business which brings me and my friend Luke to Cheyenne."

"You boys find a chair and then tell me what I can do to help."

Longarm took a seat, leaned back, and said, "You can tell me about a Scot named Ian McFain."

Foster's genial smile faded. "He's no damned good."

"He's a lot worse than that," Luke blurted out. "He's a bloody murderer!"

Marshal Foster sat up straight, eyes swinging back to Longarm. "You can prove that?"

"Yes, we can," Custis replied. "Did you hear about the murders at the Bonner Ranch?"

"Sure did! I even knew old Clyde Bonner. He'd come up here and buy some bulls every now and then, and we'd have a whiskey or two and talk about how this grass country is going to ruin because of all the damned homesteaders. Clyde Bonner was a man I liked and admired, and I was damn sad and upset when I read about him and his daughter being murdered."

"Marshal Long was engaged to Miss Bonner," Luke said. "He's killed two of the four killers, and captured a third who said that Ian McFain was the ringleader."

"Is that right, Custis?"

"Yeah. On top of that, young Josh Bonner saw the killers when they were leaving the ranch. He's described their leader, and I think that man is Ian McFain."

"Damn," Foster whispered. "I knew that Ian was a rotten apple in a barrel of sour apples, but I didn't think he was a murderer."

"Does he own a ranch a few miles north of Cheyenne?" Longarm asked.

"No. His brother, Justin, owns and operates the Bar M. Ian comes and goes as he pleases. He's never been one to put his shoulder to anything for very long. I know he's been in trouble with the law before, and when he is drinking he is tough enough to clear an entire saloon."

"I mean to find and arrest him," Longarm said flatly. "And I'll probably wind up arresting his brother as well."

"That'd be a big mistake. Justin is an invalid."

"How did that come to pass?"

"He was tossed from a horse and is paralyzed from the waist down. He's a hard but fair man with a good wife and two fine daughters. They are a nice family, and I can tell you this much for damn certain, Custis. Justin McFain did not have any part in the Bonner Ranch murders."

"Maybe not, but he must have known that his brother was the one who was responsible for those killings."

"Not necessarily. You see, Ian and Justin don't get along very well. They inherited the Bar M in equal shares, but when it became obvious to Justin that his twin brother wasn't going to do his share of the work, they had a fight. I guess Ian beat Justin pretty bad. There's been bad blood between them ever since, although Ian does come back for a spell now and then. I don't know what the financial arrangement is between the brothers, but I do know the ranch belongs to Justin alone."

Longarm steepled his fingers. "If Justin knew his brother was guilty of murder, he should have turned him over to you."

"I expect so, but—"

"And," Longarm interrupted, "if Justin accepted stolen money that came from the Bonner Ranch holdup and murders, he's going to prison. Ezra, you know that's how a judge or jury will rule."

Foster eased out of his chair and stared through his grimy front window. "Maybe you need to know some of that family's history, Custis."

Longarm didn't think past history had anything to do with murder, but he said nothing and let the older man talk.

"Ten years ago, the McFains were one of our leading families. Angus McFain homesteaded all that land to the north, and he was well liked and respected. The old man and his wife died while taking a vacation back East. I don't know what kind of affliction they contracted, but they both passed away real sudden and put this entire community in mourning."

"What has that got to do with anything?" Luke demanded. "Denver was in mourning when the Bonners were brutally murdered."

"I'm sure they were," the marshal agreed, pointing his finger down at the floor. "But we're talking about *this* situation right here and right now. You see, after Angus and his wife died, everything went downhill fast at the Bar M Ranch. Justin was by far the more responsible brother, but then he got crippled and Ian started drinking and raisin' hell. I can't tell you how many men Ian has beat up and how many wives he has . . . compromised. People up here hate and fear Ian McFain, but they generally like Justin and his family."

"How many cowboys work on the ranch?" Luke asked.

"Probably only four or five. You know, we had a terrible winter and a lot of cattle died last January. There is talk that the Bar M is going to have to be sold for back taxes and overdue debts. I hope that isn't the case. Justin McFain and his family wouldn't have a way to make a living without their ranch and cattle."

"Look," Custis said, "I don't know about Justin and all his problems. But those very same problems might be the reason that the Bonners were murdered."

"You mean to save the Bar M from going bankrupt?"

"Exactly," Longarm reasoned. "And if Justin had any knowledge of or part in planning the Bonner murders, then he's going to prison."

"He wouldn't survive a month in prison," the marshal said, his expression turning bleak. "It would be more merciful to shoot and kill Justin."

"I'm sorry," Longarm told the man. "I'm just here to uphold the law. Now, do you want to ride out in the morning and help us . . . or not?"

"I don't want to," Foster said honestly, "but I will. Maybe I should bring one of my deputies."

"I doubt that will be necessary," Longarm decided. "We don't want to ride onto the Bar M looking like a posse. What we want is for Ian to surrender peacefully. Then we'll take him down to Denver and hear what he has to say. If his brother is guilty of conspiracy to commit murder, then we'll return and make that arrest."

"All right," Foster agreed. "I'll have three horses saddled and waiting first thing tomorrow morning. Let's say eight o'clock. But when we get out to the ranch, I want to do the talking. The McFains consider me their friend. Things will go a lot smoother if it appears that I am the one in charge."

"Fair enough. We're bedding down at the Antelope Hotel. Want to have dinner with us this evening?"

"I would, but my wife has invited company over for

166

tonight. I'll just meet you out front in the morning."

Longarm started to leave, then turned and said, "I'm sorry about having to drop this trouble on you, Ezra."

"Don't give it any thought. Trouble is our business, ain't it?"

"Yeah, I guess it is at that," Longarm told the man as he headed outside with Luke on his heels.

After checking into the Antelope Hotel, Longarm and Luke had a fine steak dinner. Then Luke said, "What now?"

"I'm getting some sleep."

"I think I'll mosey around Cheyenne and maybe have a couple beers," Luke decided, looking restless.

"Suit yourself. Just don't stay up all night and drink too much. What we have to do tomorrow might call for a steady hand."

"You mean if we have to shoot Ian McFain?"

"That's right. Or we get cross-edged with his family and the Bar M cowboys."

"I hope that don't happen," Luke said. "And don't worry, I won't do any carousing. It's just that I've never been here before and I might find someone or something of interest."

"Cheyenne has plenty to offer a cowboy," Longarm said, paying their bill and then heading up to his room.

Longarm was sleeping soundly several hours later when he was awakened by the laughter and giggles. He roused himself, and looked up to see that Luke had brought two women into their hotel room. The light was poor, but there was enough of it to see the silhouettes of Luke and one of the women on the other bed doing what cowboys liked to do best to saloon girls. As if that wasn't distracting enough for a man trying to catch up on his sleep, a second woman was undressing and climbing into Longarm's bed.

"Miss," he weakly protested, "I'm just not interested tonight. Maybe next time, huh?"

167

"Honey," she said, removing the last of her clothing, "I've heard all about how your fiancée was murdered. I know you need some comforting, so just slide on over because I'm coming in to join up with you."

"But . . ."

"Honey," the young woman said, pulling back the bedcovers and easing in next to Longarm, "a big man like you needs a woman with big tits and a big heart like me to help him forget his pain and sorrows. Now you just lock your lips on one of these breasts and don't think about nothin' except what you're gonna do to Lola tonight!"

Lola did have immense breasts, and when she shoved them in Longarm's face, his lips just naturally encircled a nipple. Lola's hands were soft, and they knew how to skim lightly up and down a man's shaft until it was standing hard and at attention. Soon, very soon, sleep was the last thing on Longarm's mind.

"Now relax and let me do all the work," Lola said sweetly, throwing one of her shapely legs over his body so that her shapely bottom was poised just over his rod. "I'm going to ease down just a little bit at a time. Oh, you are big!"

"Take it slow," Longarm whispered, hearing Luke and the other woman punishing the bedsprings and breathing like a pair of racehorses.

"Oooh," Lola whispered as his throbbing shaft entered her hot womanhood. "That feels nice!"

Longarm's hips strained upward, and he moaned with pleasure because Lola felt as soft and warm inside as melted butter. Her bottom began to move up and down, then around and around.

"Lean over my mouth," he ordered, reaching for her lovely breasts as if they were clusters of succulent grapes and he was starving. Longarm took one into his mouth, and his tongue worked at her nipple until Lola started to breathe hard and her bottom began to thrust up and down faster.

"You are good," she panted. "Please, please don't come too fast."

He stopped sucking her right breast and chuckled. "You ride just as long as you want. Take it slow and easy."

But Lola didn't seem to hear him. Her head fell forward and her long, black hair swayed from side to side across Longarm's face as she rode him faster and faster. Longarm began to suck on her other breast while his hands reached up and he gripped both of her straining butt-cheeks. Finally, she sat up straight and he felt her bottom begin to twitch and jerk wildly.

"Oh, honey!" she cried. "Do it! Do it!"

He knew that Lola was losing control, and a growl born of intense pleasure formed deep in Longarm's chest as his hips began to slam upward. The fire in his rod burned until the moment when he drove his seed far up into the woman again and again. Lola moaned and collapsed forward, her womanhood sucking every last drop from his massive, thrusting tool. They lay gasping, and listened as Luke and the other woman cried out with pleasure at the climax of their own frenzied union.

After several minutes of heavy breathing, Luke chuckled and said, "I knew I could make you glad that I came along! Doesn't this beat the hell out of sleep!"

"Yeah, it does," Longarm had to agree as he smiled into the darkness.

Tired but satisfied, both Longarm and Luke were waiting for the marshal and their saddle horses at eight o'clock the following morning. Luke was impatient, pacing back and forth. "What's keeping the old man?"

"Don't worry," Longarm assured his young friend. "Foster will be here soon."

"You think we'll have to shoot Ian?"

Longarm had been considering that very question. "If

169

the Scot knows that Joe Reeves is in federal custody and will most likely talk in order to save his own neck, then I figure that McFain will fight to the death rather than surrender. What would he have to lose if he's certain to hang?"

"Nothing."

"That means he's going to be even more dangerous," Longarm told the cowboy. "It means that we take no chances."

"Would we have otherwise?"

"No," Longarm answered. "Not after what they did at the Bonner Ranch. To me, the real wild card in this deck is Justin McFain."

"He's paralyzed. Probably in a wheelchair."

"I know, but don't be fooled into thinking he can't shoot and kill us. From the waist down means he can handle a gun, and when it comes to blood . . . well, it is always thicker than water."

"I'll watch him close," Luke promised.

"Do that, and when he sees us coming, you can figure he might just have a pistol hidden on him someplace."

"Anything else I should know?"

"Only that you are forcing me to take you into a situation where you do not belong," Longarm said flatly. "It's one that could get you killed."

"We've been through that before."

"Yeah, we have. But you didn't listen, so I'm telling you one more time . . . you ought to go back to the Bonner Ranch and being a cowboy."

Luke's cheeks reddened, and he said hotly, "And I'm telling you that I'm going to stand up for Mr. Bonner and that I've decided to be a lawman!"

"More stubborn than a damned Missouri mule," Longarm muttered as Ezra Foster appeared on horseback leading two saddled horses.

"So here we go, huh?" the cowboy asked, looking excited enough to start jumping up and down in the street.

Longarm shook his head. He'd have to watch the cowboy real close, or the fool kid was going to get them into one helluva gun battle.

Chapter 20

They saw a lot of pronghorn antelope on their ride north toward the Bar M Ranch, but neither Longarm nor his two companions had much to say about them. It was an overcast day and there was a raw, whipping wind. The land was gently rolling, with deep grass and frequent buffalo wallows.

"You can just imagine what this was like fifty years ago when it was covered with buffalo," Luke said, breaking a long, tense silence. "Why, I'll bet this country was filthy with Indians. Marshal Foster?"

"Yeah?"

"Which Indians would have roamed up here?"

"Arapahoe. Pawnee. Cheyenne. Kiowa. Maybe some Sioux."

"Did they fight among themselves as much as us whites?"

"I expect. But I don't know and I really don't care. Kid, just don't open your mouth when we get to the McFain ranch house. Remember, I'm doing the talking."

"But what if they're hiding Ian in the back of the house or the barn or someplace? How you gonna know he isn't watching us down a rifle barrel?"

"I won't know," Foster snapped. "And I don't want to know. Ian and I have an understanding. I don't pick on him when he comes to town, and I don't jail him unless he's done something bad. In return, he sometimes tries to behave himself. I don't believe Ian is gonna ambush us."

Longarm wasn't of the same mind. "Ezra, I'm sure that he knows who I am and why I've come up to his brother's ranch. He'll fight before he'll surrender."

"Maybe not," the marshal of Cheyenne said in a tight voice. "He's got his brother and sister-in-law there along with them two girls to consider. Even Ian wouldn't want to put his kinfolks and them nice girls in danger."

"He *murdered* my fiancée!"

Foster twisted around in his saddle. "Now listen. I'm doing you a professional courtesy at no small risk to myself by coming out here. I'm doint it for two reasons. I like you, and I want to avoid bloodshed. So don't you be going off half cocked if Ian shows his face."

"It's a little hard not to gun a man down that murdered the woman you loved," Longarm grated. "But I'll let you handle things so long as the man surrenders to my arrest."

"He will. I'll talk to him in private, if need be."

"You do whatever you want," Longarm told the marshal. "But if what you do doesn't work, I'll take charge. I'm not leaving here without the man."

"He might already be long gone."

"I know," Longarm said. "If that's the case, you explain to his brother and sister-in-law what Ian did to the Bonner family, and then you demand that they tell you where Ian has gone."

"Don't tell me what to say or do," Foster snapped. "And I know the McFains well enough to realize that you don't 'demand' that they do anything."

"Sounds to me," Luke said quietly, "that you are kinda spooky about this bunch."

"And you sound to me like a kid who don't know his butt from a prairie-dog hole!"

"All right!" Longarm said impatiently. "Let's not start wrangling. Ezra, we've agreed that you are in charge. We'll just let it go along and see what happens."

The old marshal kicked his buckskin into a gallop, leaving Longarm and Luke behind. "Boy," Luke said, shaking his head, "he's scared to death of this family."

"He's only worried. If he were scared, Ezra would be sitting in his office chair right now instead of riding on ahead to the Bar M. Let's catch up with him."

When they trotted into the ranch yard, the first thing that Longarm saw were the two McFain girls. They were fair, with freckled cheeks and long sandy-blond hair, both skinny and in their early teens. But they weren't a bit shy, and the moment that Marshal Foster dismounted, they were grinning and giving him hugs.

The ranch house itself was modest, but in excellent repair. In addition to the house, there was the usual barn, toolshed, blacksmith shop, and tack room. Mrs. McFain must have loved flowers, for they were blowing in the wind, while chickens scratched about in a pile of old straw and manure.

"Hello, Mrs. McFain," Foster called out as he advanced up to the front porch. "How are you today?"

"I'm fine."

The woman was a larger copy of her daughters. Not pretty, but fresh and healthy-looking, with brown hair and a wide, giving smile. She wore a faded blue skirt and white blouse buttoned all the way up to her chin. Her face and arms were deeply tanned, and Longarm supposed it was because she did more than was ordinary outside, given that her husband was bound to a wheelchair.

"Ellen, is Justin inside?"

"Of course." The ranch woman studied Longarm and Luke. "Who are *they*?"

"Friends," Foster told her without bothering with introductions. "Would you ask Justin and Ian to come out?"

174

"Ian isn't here."

"Oh?"

"He left yesterday."

"Where did he go?" Foster asked.

The front door banged open and Justin McFain wheeled himself out onto the porch. He was older than Longarm would have expected, given the age of his wife. Pain or paralysis was probably the cause of his hair turning white and his cheeks being pinched and deeply lined.

"What do you want my brother for?" Justin McFain demanded, eyeing Longarm and Luke suspiciously.

"Well, Justin," Foster said, "those men behind me are from Denver. The bigger one is United States Deputy Marshal Custis Long. The other is . . . well, I guess he's a deputy or a friend of the marshal's."

"What do they want?"

"They want to talk to Ian about some trouble down south near Denver."

"He didn't do anything wrong in Colorado."

"I expect not," Marshal Foster said. "But they need to make sure. Now, can you tell me where Ian has gone?"

"Nope."

Foster turned around and glanced at Longarm, who dismounted and handed his reins to Luke, saying, "Just stay put in the saddle and don't say a word."

"Howdy," Longarm said in greeting. "Mrs. McFain. Mr. McFain. Nice ranch you have up here. We saw some of your cattle and they look good."

"What there are left of them do," McFain replied. "What is this all about anyway?"

"I just need to see your brother."

"About what?" Ellen McFain demanded. "We've a right to know."

Longarm looked at Foster. "You want to tell them . . . or should I?"

"I'll tell 'em." Foster cleared his throat. "Marshal Long believes that Ian had something to do with the murders that took place at the Bonner Ranch. Have you heard about them?"

"Sure, and my father knew and liked Clyde Bonner. What the hell would Ian have to do with that awful business!" McFain demanded, his cheeks coloring with anger. "I want you to stop beating around the bush and come right out with what you're accusing my brother of doing."

"I have evidence that he was the leader of the bunch that killed those people," Longarm said.

"Bullshit!"

"It might be that," Longarm agreed, trying to curb his own temper. "But we won't know until he has been arrested and brought before a judge who will make that decision."

McFain raised his hand and pointed it at Longarm. "And you actually expect me to believe that my own brother was behind those killings!"

"I don't care what you believe," Longarm said bluntly. "It's what a jury believes that is important."

McFain was ready to explode, but his wife laid her hand on his shoulder, saying, "Girls, go inside the house and start peeling potatoes for dinner."

"But—"

"Go on now!" McFain shouted. "Don't you be arguing with your mother."

The girls hurried inside, and when the door was open for a moment, Longarm tried to see inside to learn if Ian McFain was lying in wait. But the interior of the ranch house was too dim.

"Listen," Foster said, "I don't want any trouble."

"Then maybe you ought to leave right now," McFain snapped.

"We can't do that," Longarm said. "At least, not until we are sure that your brother is gone."

"Why, you—"

"Justin!" Ellen McFain knelt at her husband's side. "This could get ugly and there are the girls to think of.

176

Why don't we just let these men take a look in the house and around the place. Then they can leave in peace."

"No!"

"Please. Let's not have any trouble. Not with the law."

Longarm waited, watching the rancher's ravaged face. It was clear that the man was suffering and in pain. It was equally clear that he was enraged by what he considered an invasion and an injustice. But his wife was calm and she had authority. McFain gave in to both.

"All right, dammit! Come inside and have your look. Then go around the place and prove me a liar."

"Justin," Foster said, "I'm real sorry. You know I liked your father and I've great respect for you and your family. But these men have come a long way and it's best to satisfy them. Otherwise, they'd just keep coming back to pester you."

"Then git to your damn business!" the rancher shouted.

Longarm turned to Luke and said, "You stay put."

"Yes, sir."

"I'll show you into the house," Ellen McFain told Longarm. "Follow me."

"Much obliged, ma'am."

The inspection of the McFain house was quick, but Longarm made sure that it was thorough. He looked in the closets, under the beds, and in the root cellar located just behind the house near the kitchen.

"Any attic up there?"

"No."

Longarm studied the ceiling and could see no evidence that the woman was lying. He hated to look into the girls' room, but he did, and they watched him with wide, solemn eyes. After that, he went outside, knelt in the dirt, and peered under the porch, but saw nothing.

"If you think my brother is the kind to hide in the dirt, you are sadly mistaken," Justin McFain told him.

"Luke, hand over the reins and let's go check the barn, bunkhouse, and other outbuildings."

Luke seemed pleased that he was finally going to play some small role. He gave the reins to Marshal Foster, then started to draw his side arm, but McFain bellowed, "You keep that gun holstered, gawdammit!"

"Do as he says," Longarm instructed.

Luke dropped his gun as if the handle was hot. He followed Longarm silently to the barn, then through the other buildings. The only living things they saw were horses in the back corral and a sick cowboy in the bunkhouse.

"I got the measles and a terrible fever," the Bar M employee told them. "So better stay clear if you ain't had 'em already."

"Hey, cowboy, I sure hope you get to feeling better soon," Luke told the kid who looked to be no older than himself.

"Thanks. What's going on?"

"We're looking for Ian McFain."

"He rode over to Laramie just yesterday to gamble and raise hell. Probably comin' back in a few days."

Longarm just caught the remark on his way out of the bunkhouse, but didn't say a word. Instead, he marched back to Foster and McFain and said, "Mr. McFain, where did your brother go?"

"Beats me."

"I'll just bet it does," Longarm growled. "Marshal Foster, we can leave now."

"Get them the hell off'a my land," McFain hissed. "And you'd better not bring 'em back or I won't be so civil next time!"

It was all Longarm could do to keep his silence as he mounted his horse, reined it hard around, and spurred away.

Chapter 21

As soon as they were off the Bar M Ranch, Longarm reined his horse up and said, "Ezra, we thank you for your help back there."

"You're welcome," Foster answered. "Sorry that we didn't get your man."

"That's all right," Longarm replied. "We're heading for Laramie."

Foster frowned. "Why?"

"Because there was a sick cowboy in the bunkhouse and he told us that's where Ian McFain went."

Foster blinked. "How come you didn't say so earlier?"

"Because the cowboy was sick and I doubt him telling us what he did would have set well with Justin McFain."

"No," Foster said, "I doubt it would have at that. What ailed the cowboy?"

"He said he had the measles."

"Holy shit! That's what one of my deputies has right now, and he's been sick for nearly a week. I ain't sure if I had the measles as a kid or not."

Longarm said, "I had 'em already."

"Me too," Luke added.

"I'm heading back to Cheyenne," Foster decided. "I sure

hope I don't get the measles at my age. Might kill me. Wouldn't that be somethin', considering all the scrapes I've fought?"

Longarm nodded and the old marshal spurred his horse into a gallop, heading back down to Cheyenne.

"He's quite a fella, ain't he," Luke said. "But he ought to hand his badge over to a younger man."

"Probably so," Longarm agreed. "Now, let's go find Ian McFain and bring him to justice."

"Or kill him."

They had not ridden thirty miles when they saw a rider approaching them from the direction of Laramie.

"If we're lucky, that might be our man," Longarm said, spurring his horse forward.

They were galloping stirrup to stirrup when the oncoming rider finally noticed them. By then, Longarm was certain the man was Ian McFain because he was large and he wore a long red and green scarf or sash around his neck and a cap on his head.

"Luke, fall back!" Longarm shouted as he drew his gun and charged ahead.

When the Scot saw them coming, he also drew his side arm, bellowed an oath, and spurred his own horse forward. As the gap closed between them, Longarm didn't waste his breath to shout for the Scot to surrender. Instead he took aim, fired, and missed.

The Scot opened fire as well, and then Luke overtook Longarm, riding like the devil on the fastest of the three horses.

"Luke, no!" Longarm bellowed, struggling to get more speed out of his flagging mount, but the cowboy kept going.

Longarm saw fire and smoke spurt from the Scot's gun two more times just before Luke drove his horse into the killer's mount, knocking both animals to the earth and spilling the riders hard.

Moments later, Longarm reached the spot and vaulted from his horse. "Luke, are you all right?" he asked, kneeling by the cowboy's side.

The young man raised up, then suddenly knocked Longarm aside as the Scot fired across twenty yards of prairie grass. Longarm rolled, extended his gun hand, took deadly aim, and pulled the trigger three times in rapid succession. The Scot died on his knees screaming curses at the sky.

"Luke!"

The cowboy brought his blood-covered hand up from his side. He gulped and whispered, "I never been shot before. Marshal, am I about to die?"

Longarm quickly examined a flesh wound so deep and nasty that he could see shattered ribs. "No, Luke, you won't die, but you aren't going to be riding any broncs for a while."

"Then how about us holin' up at the Antelope Hotel for a few nights with them lusty gals before we head back down to Denver? I can still ride one of *them,* can't I?"

Longarm shook his head and said in his most solemn voice, "Kid, that bullet traveled down your side and you're not exactly a steer. . . . but you ain't exactly a bull either."

"Oh, no!" Luke cried, tearing at his belt buckle and then at his pants. But after a quick inspection of his privates, he relaxed, and then even managed to chuckle. "Dammit, you sure fooled me a good'un that time. But I have to know . . . did I finally prove myself lawman material this time?"

"You did," Longarm replied, thinking about how this fool kid had probably just saved his life. "Now all we got to do is convince my boss, Billy Vail, that you're gonna make a fine United States deputy marshal."

Luke's handsome face split into a wide grin. "You're gonna do that for me?"

"Why not? After what I've just witnessed, you must be the luckiest man I've ever known."

"Why lucky? I got shot, didn't I?"

"Yeah," Longarm admitted, "but you're still alive, and damned if I can figure out why."

Longarm bandaged the cowboy's shattered ribs, then caught up the horses. He muscled Ian McFain's body across his saddle and lashed him down tight. Then he helped Luke into the saddle and mounted his own horse, turning his gaze to the south, toward Colorado.

"You know, Luke. We could ride back to Cheyenne and go through all the hullabaloo concerned with transporting a body by train across state lines, or we could just head for Denver and keep things simple. Are you up for riding that far?"

"Sure, but if we did that, we'd have to pass up them two lusty Cheyenne women."

Longarm shook his head. "I got a feeling you'll find us a couple more soon after we reach Denver."

"You got *that* right," Luke said with a sly but pained grin.

Watch for

LONGARM AND THE LOVE SISTERS

264th novel in the exciting LONGARM series
from Jove

Coming in November!

LONGARM

Explore the exciting Old West with one of the men who made it wild!

J. R. ROBERTS
THE
GUNSMITH